Introduction

I released this book to prove   ns
you have (and we all have the
overcome anything if you kee
your way.

I, myself, have special needs and development problems. It
took me over ten years of writing, disappointments, and
obstacles to write and release my first story, this story!

Therefore, with me trying to get across this message:
**Parts of this book may lead to a flurry of emotions. If
you feel yourself getting overwhelmed, please consider
taking a couple of days break from the story before
going back to it.**

Just Keep Fighting!!

This story is a fictional work with non-fictional elements. It's
not a true story for me personally, but things like this will
happen to people in really life.

I hope you enjoy Relate. Any feedback can be sent to the
email address or the social media pages in the 'About Me'
section at the end. Thanks for picking up my first story!

Shane, author of Relate.

1

My Name is Freddy Lewis. I was brought up by my Uncle Andy and never really knew my parents. Something else I never knew was how great having a brother would be. In fact, I am lying there: Ever since I was about eight, I have wanted a little brother, somebody that could look up to me, that I could inspire! It would have also been nice to have someone to play with. Sure, I had a couple of friends, but that did not seem the same, especially watching my friends with their brothers and sisters. I used to make up siblings in the stories I wrote so I would not feel so lonely. Of course, as soon as I closed the story, it was back to reality.

My Uncle would play with me and keep me company when he could but was working all the time whilst I was growing up. I attend Portsmouth College and have lived in the city all my life. I am really enjoying the course I am doing, and the tutors are great and know their stuff. I am currently doing a computer course but am thinking of moving to a creative writing course at the college in September.

It was a sunny day and I came into my house. I found my uncle in his bedroom when I went upstairs. I gave him a hug. "Hey Freds, how did it go today?" Uncle Andy asked. 'Freds' is my uncle's nickname for me. No one else can call me it. I like people to use my full name: Freddy rather than Fred, etc. My uncle, of course, is different and became a sign of the great bond we have.

"It went great, I'm doing very well on my coursework! At least, I think I am" I added.
"Well, if there was a problem, your tutor would talk to you about it"
"Oh thanks, he's calling me in early tomorrow morning, says he has something important to discuss with me!" I informed

him. "I knew this would happen!".

Uncle Andy pulled me onto the bed beside him. He wrapped an arm around my shoulder.

"Remember what we've spoken about. Take each day and each problem as it comes along. We do not even know if there is a problem yet. If there is, we'll work on it and I'm sure Danny will help you too" Uncle Andy said calmly. Danny McKeen is my college tutor.

Uncle Andy and I talked for about fifteen minutes before I went downstairs and made us both a sandwich. I had coursework to complete so I did so in my room while I ate and listened to music. As much as I love working with computers, I just have this huge passion for music. I always wanted to learn how to play numerous instruments, but I could not ever decide which ones.

I also like to sing, although my next-door neighbour does not like me doing so! Although Uncle Andy smiles when I sing, you do not have to be a physic to know that he does not like my singing voice either. I used to be a brilliant singer growing up but then my vocals dropped like a Hardwell beat, it turned my voice into a squealing dog! I think Uncle Andy likes me singing due to the fact I only sing now when I am really happy.

I had completed my coursework by 7p.m., I just could not get this meeting out of my head! Although I knew students are not supposed to engage with their tutors on social media, I had to know if I was in trouble. I sent Danny a message via Facebook:

'Hey Danny, Sorry I know I'm not supposed to message you on here. Can you please just tell me if I'm in any trouble at the meeting tomorrow? I can't get it out of my mind. Thanks!'.

I went down the hall at about 7:30p.m. to see Uncle Andy. He had just gotten a bath.

"Anything good on telly?" I asked him. He shrugged and grabbed for the remote to check.

"By the way, I've messaged my tutor to find out more about tomorrow. I told him I'm sorry for breaking the social media rule, but I was desperate to find out more" I told Uncle Andy. He nodded and smiled.

"Yeah, that is a reasonable and great idea. Mind you, you have always had the reasoning brain, ever since you were little" Uncle Andy told me, with a smile.

"Uncle Andy, why will you never tell me what happened to my parents and why I had to come and live with you?" I asked.

He stared at me, although I could see that he was not at all surprised that I had asked. I was sat on the edge of the bed.

"Alright. I'll tell you as much as I can at this moment: You came to live with me when you were just under three years old, as you already know. Your Mum and Dad were good people, but something happened, not really bad but it changed them. They started taking some bad stuff..." Uncle Andy started.

"Drugs?" I suspected. He nodded.

"Some really nasty ones too. And it affected them looking after you. One time, they forgot to take you off the bus with them and you ended up in London. I had to go to collect you" Uncle Andy explained.

"Anyway...In the end, I'd had enough and reported them to Social Services myself. They came and took you away. I was given temporary custody of you until the hearing, which is known as being a foster parent. When it came to the hearing, neither of your parents turned up, sent any representatives, or even put in any defence case. When that's the case, usually the foster carer, which is me gets granted full custody, if the foster carer accepts. This happened in your case. I of course, became your adoptive parent. I have offered your parents contact with you about 40 times over the years, but I eventually gave up. The last thing I ever wanted was you getting hurt" Uncle Andy explained, his face and tone full of sympathy and sensitivity. I nodded and gave him a long hug.

I had of course been having questions about my parents for at least a decade, which is apparently natural for a kid who hardly knew his parents,

My tutor got back to me on Facebook. The laptop read: '21:01'.
'Hi Freddy, that's fine and I must apologise for not telling you more about our little meeting tomorrow. You're not in trouble in the slightest, in fact you will be involved in the start of an exciting project we are taking on! Will explain everything when I see you tomorrow. Due to our college's safeguarding procedures, I will have to file a screenshot of what we've said in this message. See you tomorrow at around 9am' Danny had put.
I just put back: 'Thanks and I have no problem with that'
Now I was not nervous or scared, I was excited.

I went downstairs and talked some more with Uncle Andy for about half an hour while he was cleaning the kitchen a bit. I was yawning my head off!
"I didn't know I was THAT boring!" Uncle Andy teased me. I stuck my tongue out at him. We said good night to each other before I took a glass of water upstairs to my room. I got changed into my pyjamas and shut my laptop down. I looked out of the window for a long minute, just staring outside. Closing my curtains, I climbed into bed and got ready to sleep.

2

The next morning, I woke up at around 7:20a.m. I sat up and stretched my arms and legs. I got ready for college, wearing my usual style which consists of smart black trousers and usually a bright coloured T-shirt. Today, I put on my favourite Doctor Who one. It has a silhouette of the Ninth Doctor, my favourite incarnation of the Timelord! They are quite rare, my uncle found it about three years ago. Luckily, I have always grown very slowly! I knocked on my uncle's bedroom door.

"Come in" Uncle Andy shouted. I opened the door. Uncle Andy had just finished getting dressed. We exchanged good mornings.

"Did Danny ever get back to you last night?" Uncle Andy asked me. I nodded.

"Oh yeah. He said I'm not in trouble and it's just about a new project they want me to be a part of. He said he'll explain everything this morning. He asked for me to be there for about 9a.m., Everyone else is getting 9:30a.m." I explained to my Uncle.

He nodded and smiled at me.

"I told you there was nothing to worry about" He said.

I nodded and thanked him for his support.

"That's what I'm here for!" He said.

We walked downstairs together and had some breakfast. I had Shreddies and Coco Pops.

"I still don't get how you can eat mixed cereals" He said to me.

"Easy" I exclaimed, taking a mouthful of cereal. "See?" I joked. He rolled his eyes.

I laughed.

We ate our cereal in silence. I helped him to clean and dry all the pots. Uncle Andy then had to go to work in his tiny office. He started working from home about six months ago and was loving it! I went into my room and made sure it was tidy and made my bed.

I left the house after telling Uncle Andy I'd be home between three and four o'clock. The hallway clock now read: '08:35', with the college a fifteen-minute walk away through some outstanding greenery. I got to the college site around ten minutes early and waited for Danny to come out of the staff room he shared with three other tutors.

Danny came out and greeted me with a smile on his face. "Hey Freddy, how are you doing this morning?" He asked. "I'm doing great thanks. I'm just keen on hearing more about this project you were talking about" I replied honestly. He laughed and nodded understandingly.

"Well, I guess I'll get straight to it then! The college has given us some space and funding for a little booth like shop near the café downstairs. As you might have seen, we have decided to turn it into a computer repair shop. It'll be open to students, staff and even members of the public. Since you're one of the most friendly and polite people I know, I would love it if you would do the first ever shift!" Danny revealed to me. I looked back at him with shock and amazement.

"It may be a good idea to keep that last bit about you being one of the nicest quiet from your classmates!" He added. I nodded and promised I would not tell them.
"This sounds great thanks. All I want to do is help people and with this shop thing, I can train more and help others at the same time" I exclaimed. Danny Smiled and nodded.
"My thoughts exactly, and all the work is going to be free so it really will be helping people!" He said.
"Yes, I'd love to!" I accepted the offer. Danny shook my hand.
"Each person working a shift will earn a lunch voucher for

that day. They also get to own their very own jumper of my own design" Danny explained. I nodded and said that would be great. I was really looking forward to this! The morning went by quite slowly, although I still enjoyed it.

At lunch, Danny bought me my lunch using the department's budget then led me to the booth to show me everything. It looked like a real shop. Well, I guess it is! The guys had just fitted the shutters and were giving Danny the keys.
"Why don't you be the first to open the shutter?" My tutor asked. I thanked him and took the keys. I opened the shutter, lifted the screen gate and the counter so we could get in. We had a look around and he showed me how to use the computer cataloguing system. He also recapped data protection, health and safety and general rules.

"It's awfully dirty in here...How would you like to earn a bottle of Fanta". He looked around. "Or two?" My tutor asked. I laughed. I was always drinking Fanta.
"Go on then. Hold up, there's some cleaning supplies in this little cupboard here! I'll get cleaning this place and I will see you later" I said to the tutor. He nodded and thanked me again. Whilst Danny went off to plan his lesson for this afternoon, I started scrubbing at the grime underneath the desks. I worked at cleaning for about fifteen minutes. I heard footsteps approaching the booth.

Despite expecting them to walk by like they usually would do, they stopped right outside the counter.
"Erm, Hello?" A woman's voice called in. I wrinkled up my nose and showed myself from under the counter.
"Hi there, I was wondering if you could help get my laptop back up and running please?" The woman asked.
"Well, we don't actually open till Monday. I'm just cleaning it today. I will be working in here a lot though so maybe I might be able to do this one early. Let's start again: what's wrong with it?" I asked her.

"Oh, thanks for that. Sorry to bother you early, just I need it for work, so it is kind of urgent. My name's Amy Jamme by the way" Amy told me. I nodded and smiled.

"I'm Freddy, Freddy Lewis. I'm happy to help!" I exclaimed.

"I'm not sure what's going on with it but it's just going really slow up to the point when it won't do anything. I think the term...Crashed, is right?" Amy explained. I nodded.

"Yep, that's a proper term. Good job! Anyway, it sounds like it could do with an internal clean-up and a virus and malware scan. It won't affect any of your files, although we'd always highly recommend backing your files up on an alternative device like a USB stick" I explained my ideas on the problems.

"I'd be happy with that, thanks. How much do I pay for this?" Amy inquired.

"All the work is provided for free since we're all training!" I explained to the woman. She nodded and thanked me again.

"I'm not one hundred percent sure on how to complete a backup and I'm late for a meeting. So, did you say to bring it back on Monday?" Amy asked.

I thought for a moment.

"You can do, or...I could have a look now, including the back up. We do sell memory sticks here. I'm not really meant to perform the backup, but I doubt it'll be a problem!" I told her. I launched the shops computer and loaded up the cataloguing system. I asked Amy to fill in her details on to a paper form. She paid for the memory stick and I took the laptop in and set it up. Once Amy had completed the form, I put it aside, out of view.

"That's great thanks. I'll let you get off to your meeting. I'll ring you when I have an update" I informed her.

"See you later!" She said before running off.

I put her and her laptop's details into the system. Turning

on the customer's computer, I waited for it to load. I plugged in my own external hard drive with the cleaning software on. It took fifteen minutes to load! Finally, I managed to get onto disk cleaner. I checked all the options and pressed enter. I also completed disk defrags and the virus scans. It did take over an hour but could see the difference, which is what makes it all worth it.

I could see Danny coming up to the counter.
"What's taking so long?" He asked.
"Erm..." I started. He looked into the shop.
"You've started already?" Danny asked me, I could tell he was a bit shocked.
"Yeah, this woman came up and I could tell she was desperate. She said she needs it for work" I explained.

Danny nodded.
"So...How is it going?" He asked.
"Actually, I've just about done all I can, and you can really tell the difference, although it's not perfect" I admitted to my tutor.
"Well remember, we can only do so much. Computers unfortunately diminish with age, even with the best care. It might be a sad sight, but it happens. A little thing to remember is that there is no such thing as perfect, everyone and everything has their faults which help to shape us" Danny reminded me. I nodded. He looked at Amy's laptop himself.
"You've done a great job Freddy! And this is for you" He said handing me a jumper.

"Thanks, and this jumper looks great!" I exclaimed. He smiled.
"You can stay down here if you want, that's entirely up to you? I'm happy with your written work" Danny offered.
I nodded and said I would like to stay in the shop until home time. He left for the classroom after saying farewell to me.

I put the thick black jumper on. Whilst Amy's laptop did one last scan, I went back to cleaning the shop. After about ten minutes, the special jumper began to feel as if it had a bee's nest shoved up it. I tried scratching the feeling away, but that seemed to make it even worse. Amy walked up as I was jigging around trying to make the itching go away.

I stopped suddenly when I saw her. She laughed.
"How's it going?" She asked, with a smile. I walked up to the counter.
"Sorry about that. The laptop is definitely a lot better than it was and you should be able to use it properly now. I've set up both the clean ups and the virus scans so that they will automatically scan your laptop every week which should help the computer to stay as healthy as possible" I explained. Suddenly the itching sensation seemed to come back to me, but this time a thousand times worse. Nearly screaming, I tugged the jumper off me and threw it to the floor and kicked it to the other side.
"Oh my god, your skin!" Amy gasped. As I had tugged the jumper off, my T-shirt had lifted, showing my bare skin. The skin was red, but I said I would be okay in a bit.

"Thanks so much for that, I really do appreciate it!" Amy said to me, picking up her laptop bag. I smiled.
"It was a pleasure!" I said.
"I should have noticed it before, but my son would love your shirt! The Ninth Doctor is his favourite!" She exclaimed.
"Mine too-But you might have already guessed that!" I said laughing. She shared the laugh.
"Was that your son on the screensaver?" I enquired.

Amy nodded.
"Technically speaking, I adopted William as a baby. Apparently, his parents had a really bad history with drugs, so the authorities took him away straight away. They'd lost one kid already years before. They've never even bothered

with him or tried to see him!" She explained, getting very emotional. I passed her a tissue; she thanked me and dabbed her eyes.

"Anyway, why am I telling you all this. You don't want to know about it all!" Amy exclaimed. I smiled understandably at her and said I did not mind.

"Wait a minute, you said these parents already had a kid taken off them?" I asked. She nodded.

"And they did drugs?"

"Yep, disgusting I know!" She exclaimed.

"Oh god!" I said suddenly. She stared at me.

"Can't be?" I exclaimed. I forgot for a moment where I was and of the woman in front of me.

"Erm, sorry Amy, was just thinking about something" I told her.

"What do you mean?" She asked me with interest.

"What happened to this other kid?" I asked.

"We are not sure, apparently he went to live with a relative or something, for some reason my minds saying an uncle? I was told about this through friends so don't know how much truth there is in this" Amy informed me. I put a hand over my face.

"Oh god, what have we done?" I muttered.

"Erm, Amy, I think there's a chance I am William's brother!" I revealed. She looked at me shocked.

"My uncle gained custody of me when I was three. My biological parents, I've been told, did some really bad drugs, and got into a lot of trouble. They haven't bothered with me neither" I explained.

Amy was stuck in thought. I waited for her to say something.

"What did you say your surname was?" She asked me.

"Freddy Lewis is my full name. I believe it's the one I was born with too" I told her.

She paced around the counter. She looked at me.

"You ARE his brother! Lewis was his original surname..." Amy exclaimed with a gasp.

I stared at her and she stared back at me, neither of us obviously knew what to do next. Danny walked up to us.

"Err, Danny, may I go home please. I have something I need to take in and think about!" I asked my tutor. Danny looked at me for a moment.

"Sure, are you okay?" He asked me with concern.

"Why wouldn't I be?" I said. I near enough flew out of the college, forgetting my coat, forgetting about the traffic. I ran into my house and to my bedroom. I slammed the door and hid under my computer desk. I wrapped my arms around my legs and tried to control my mind.

3

About five minutes later, there was a knock on my bedroom door.
"Freds, you okay?" Uncle Andy asked through the door. Although I obviously could not see him, I could hear pure concern in his voice.

We had a rule that if I were angry or needed space, Uncle Andy would leave me five minutes and then come and check on me. I looked up at the door from my place under the desk.
"Yeah...I don't know" I admitted.
"May I come in please?" Uncle Andy asked.
"Yeah, okay" I said. My uncle opened the door and walked up to me, ducking down so we were eye to eye.
"What's wrong bud?" He asked. I looked at him.

"I've got a brother" I told him, looking down at my feet.
Uncle Andy stared at me.
"Okay, what's brought this on then?" He asked me.
"The reason why Danny called me in early today was the college has opened a computer repair shop open to the public. Technically speaking, it was meant to open next Monday. As I was cleaning the place, this woman came up to the booth with her laptop. I couldn't just leave it, so I accepted it in early" I started. Uncle Andy nodded and motioned for me to continue.
"Well, I fixed the problem the best I could, and the computer is now working great. Anyway, she came back, and we get talking" I went on.

"I see, what got you from there to suspecting this?" Uncle Andy asked honestly.

"As we were talking, she mentioned how her son would love my T-shirt and how the Ninth Doctor is his favourite too. She had a photo of a boy as her screensaver. I just asked her if that was her son and she said it was. Then she blurted out how she had in fact adopted him as a baby, she got quite emotional about it all. Anyway, during that she said how his parents had been bad druggies, they'd already had one kid taken away a while back and that neither of the parents had bothered to contact or see him" I concluded.

"That doesn't mean it's definitely you though. I know it isn't a good fact but there are lots of people who take bad things" My uncle exclaimed.
I stared at him for a long moment and shook my head.
"She then asked me to tell her my full name again and once I did so, she confirmed that I am the kid's brother. His name's William. The family are called the Jammes'" I explained.

He took a long deep breath.
"You say you've found out that you have a brother. So, I have one question for you: Why are you running away from it?" Uncle Andy asked me sympathetically. I stared back at him.
"Because...Because I'm scared! More scared than I've ever been!" I cried. He nodded.
"That's understandable Freds" He said quietly.
"What do I do?" I asked him.
My uncle sighed, stood up and moved over to my bed and sat down on the edge.

"You've always said you wanted a brother or a sister. It's all I heard whilst you were growing up and now you have one! Don't you owe it to yourself and to him to try and give it a go?" Uncle Andy asked.

"I don't know if she or even he wants anything to do with me. As soon as she gave me the news I ran straight out of the college and never looked back till I got home" I told my uncle. He looked back at me and signalled for me join him on the bed beside him.

I slowly followed it.
"You've just been told something that could change your life forever. Of course, you ran or tried to get away. Next time you see this woman, ask if you can sit down privately with her and talk with her and...just see what you both think" Uncle Andy recommended with a faint smile.
I smiled back and nodded at him.

Uncle Andy and I then had some tea together before he went to lay down on his bed for a bit. I got Facebook Messenger notification. I saw that I had a message request. I clicked on it and found it to be from Amy Jamme!
'Hi Freddy, I understand why you ran away today so don't hold that against yourself. It was a massive discovery for both of us! No pressure but this message is just so if you ever want to meet up, just you and me and discuss everything, you know you can contact me here. Thanks, and was lovely to meet you today' The message read. I stared at the message, repeating it in my mind again and again. I decided to follow my heart.

With a shaky finger, I accepted the message request and replied:
'Hi Amy, it was a pleasure meeting you today. I'm sorry I ran like that. It took my uncle to get me to admit to myself that I was scared and nervous. I would like to meet up with you as soon as we can, so we can work everything out, although I do want to take any arrangements slowly and ease into it. Hope you're well?'.

I decided to listen to some music on my laptop.

Amy got back to me at around 8p.m. and we had this conversation:
Amy: 'I understand and thanks so much for getting back to me. I know it must have taken a lot of courage for you to do so! Of course, we'll take it at whatever speed we want to! I'm free to meet you tomorrow at a café or something?'.
Me: 'You're welcome. I think I owe it to myself and William to see what we should do. I can come closer to you if you want. Where do you live?'.
Amy: 'Southsea, near Milton school'.
Me: 'I know of it. Do you want to meet at Canoe Lake, I used to enjoy going there as a kid? I haven't been for a while'.
Amy: 'That'll be great thanks! What time do you wanna say?'.
Me: 'Maybe around 11:30ish?'.
Amy: 'Sounds cool. I've got until 3pm anyway so that'd give us plenty of time. My husband is taking William to his cousin's birthday party who live in Bristol! When I say cousin, it's one of my brother's children, as I said, we don't really know anyone from William's biological family. I will see you there and meet you at the entrance gates'.

We finished confirming the plans and said farewells before I went downstairs. I had a munch on some biscuits and poured myself a glass of milk. After about fifteen minutes, I decided that I had probably had enough and went back upstairs and went down the landing to Uncle Andy's bedroom.

The door was open so walked straight in. He was now watching telly and smiled when he saw me.
"Me and Amy are meeting in Southsea tomorrow. Canoe Lake" I informed my uncle. He looked at me and turned off the telly immediately.

"Right. Is that where they live then?" He asked. I nodded. "I'm meeting her there at 11:30a.m." I told my uncle, "Her husband is taking William to a birthday party in Bristol, so it will just be me and her this time. I'm actually really looking forward to it!". Uncle Andy smiled and gave me a big hug.

"Well done Freds!" He congratulated me.
"Thanks Uncle Andy!" I replied.
"I want you to listen to me. No matter what happens...No matter where this new chapter takes you, I will always be there for you. Do not ever forget that. You will always be my nephew" Uncle Andy told me. I nodded.
"No one could replace you!" I promised him. He smiled and nodded. Uncle Andy said he was getting really tired, so I said good night and left him to go to sleep. I got us both glasses of water and decided to call it an early night myself.

4

I woke up at around 8a.m. all refreshed. Remembering what I was to be doing today, I had quickly decided to get bathed and dressed up ready for our meeting. I was not thinking like a blazer or anything, just a smart shirt with the usual smart black trousers. I climbed out of bed and went to see Uncle Andy. The door was open again, this time my uncle was not in his room. I went downstairs and looked around the house. I found him doing some washing in the utility room.

"Morning Freds. How are you on this fine day?" Uncle Andy asked me.
"I'm cool thanks. Kinda excited about today...and nervous!" I admitted to my uncle. He nodded understandingly.
"You're doing it though, for which I'm really proud of you. There's no rush to jump straight into anything" He reminded me. I nodded slowly.

Whilst Uncle Andy finished loading and unloading washing into the washer and dryer, I went to the kitchen and had some breakfast. I felt even more alert and cheerful as soon as I took my first spoonful. It was now 9:15a.m., I went into the bathroom, taking my smart clothes in with me. I admit, I think I spent around an hour bathing, spraying, and making sure I looked smart and neat! I wanted this woman to keep a great impression of me. I wanted Amy to know that I was a good, caring but fun person.

I tidied my room up for a bit. By the time I went to see my

uncle again, it was around 10:30a.m. It suddenly hit me that this was really happening! I would be setting off to meet up with the adoptive parent of my brother in half an Hour!

Uncle Andy was tiding up his bedroom.
"How are you feeling about today?" He asked me, smiling.
"I'm very excited!" I exclaimed.
"Well, I'm going to get you a taxi going there. I wanted to show you how proud I was of you and I think this might make it all a bit easier for you" My uncle revealed. I nodded and thanked him. Uncle Andy double checked that he had enough for the journey before I called the taxi company up.

I booked the taxi for 11a.m. The journey from my house to Canoe Lake should take around 15 minutes, but I wanted to make sure I was there on time. I went into my room and collected some of my pocket money. My uncle still gives me a bit of money every week for doing jobs for him and for 'Being myself', although I have told him there's no need. I left my room and wandered back to my uncle's room.
"I'm coming down to see you off" He explained. I smiled.
"Hope you have a fantastic time and...Just be yourself!" Uncle Andy told me. I nodded and thanked him again. With good timing, the moment arrived. Not with a bang, but with a horn. The taxi was here.

I got into the front passenger seat and my uncle stood at the door and waved me off. When my uncle was out of sight, the driver spoke to me.
"So, where you going to mate?" He asked.
"Canoe Lake in Southsea please. Just near the main entrance gates" I told the Driver. He nodded and typed the destination into his sat nav.

"Doing anything nice there?" He asked, making

conversation while still concentrating on the roads.

"I recently found out that I have a brother and I'm meeting his adoptive Mum" I explained.

"When did all this start?" He asked.

"Yesterday. I am doing a computer course at college and we have opened a repair shop that's open to the public. She came in having problems with a laptop. We got talking and eventually, it turned out that I was her kid's brother. I'd been taken off those same parents as he had when I was three and went to live with my uncle. I actually cannot remember them at all!" I blurted. Now I was blurting stuff out!

"Hope it goes well for you then!" The taxi driver said. I smiled and thanked him.

About ten minutes later, we were moving through Southsea towards Canoe Lake. Traffic up to this point had been okay but it was now starting to build up a bit. Surprisingly, it did not seem to slow the journey down and we were opposite the gates by 11:20a.m.

"So, that'll be £5.40 please?" The driver asked cheerfully. I reached into my pocket.

"Keep the change" I said, giving him six pound in pound coins.

"Thanks!" He said, "Have a great time!".

"You too" I replied, before getting out and closing the door. The taxi drove off, leaving me standing at the side of the road. Leaving me staring at my future.

My mouth suddenly felt dry and the dryness was dripping down my throat, so I ran into a shop and got a small bottle of water. I sat down on a nearby bench, taking small sips of the water and taking slow, deep breaths. I knew that I was just feeling nervous and that I would feel better once Amy and I started talking. I looked at my phone and saw it read: '11:28'. Taking one last deep breath, I stood up and walked across the road. I stepped up to the entrance gates of Canoe Lake.

Canoe Lake is a popular attraction for all ages. However, most of the time outside of school holidays, it is peaceful and a great place to relax, hang out and grab a drink at the café. Being true to its name, Canoe Lake features a lake where you can loan canoes and peddle boats.

I saw a car coming towards me on the main road. It honked at me. Then I saw the driver waving to me. Amy. There were parking bays along the side of the road. She pulled into one. She got out and got a ticket from a parking machine nearby. I then heard click of automatic locks.
"Hi Freddy, I'm sorry if I'm late" She said, walking up to me. I smiled.
"No problem at all. It actually gave me a minute to stop butterflies making their way up my throat" I joked. She laughed.
"Are you feeling okay about doing this?" Amy asked.
"Sure I am. Apart from feeling a bit nervous, I am mostly excited to find out more" I admitted to her. She smiled.
"You haven't met him yet" She joked. We shared a laugh.

We walked into Canoe Lake.
"Do you want to get a drink or something to eat? My treat!" She asked me, looking at the café ahead of us.
"Yeah, that'd be great. I've brought some money for myself..." I started.
"It's staying in your pocket. The least I can do is treat you to something after you agreed to come all the way down here" Amy told me. I nodded and thanked her; I didn't want to argue with her.

We strolled along to the café. It wasn't too busy, and we found two leather sofas and a low coffee table in the corner. We sat down opposite one another.

"Take a look at the left side of each page on the menu, not the right, and tell me what you'd like" Amy said to me.

"Okay, thanks very much!" I replied. We looked at the menu for about five minutes. I decided to get a cheese and ham toastie with a banana milkshake. I, of course, asked Amy if that was okay.

"Of course, it is! You'd need to spend about £50 more to catch up with him!" She told me. I laughed. Amy ordered the food at the counter before coming back over to me.

"So, tell me about William and you guys" I asked with interest. She smiled.

"Well as you know his name is William. He's ten. We're so close, you wouldn't tell William was adopted. He was only a baby when he came to live with us" Amy explained.

"One thing I must add though. I promise I will never replace any of you guys and don't want to" I told Amy. She smiled.

"That's great but I know you wouldn't. William wouldn't let you anyway! Actually, I haven't told him yet-About you. I decided I'd tell him tonight if we both agree to go ahead" She exclaimed.

I nodded and agreed.

"So, if William had to move to a desert island for a month, what five things would he take...Not counting essential food and drink?" I asked Amy, trying a fun way of finding out more.

"Does that include the Wi-Fi?" She said, rolling her eyes. I laughed.

"I'd say: His toy vehicles, his tablet, Goosebumps books, his best friend if he can. There's too many to mention but you get the idea!" Amy informed me.

"I never had a tablet when I was younger, but I spent hours playing with my cars and buses, most of my cars were like traders one like Walkers and juice vans." I explained.

"I'm sure he'd love to see them, he's into that kind of stuff!" She told me. I nodded.

"Eh, sure. I'll have a look and see what I can find when I get in!" I offered.

"Thanks! Now that's enough about my little monster, what was you like?" She asked. I laughed.

"Short, chubby, geeky, need I go on?" I joked.

"Yes please!" She replied. I stuck my tongue out at her.

"I was mainly quiet, but with many moments of loud and fun mixed in. I have always liked learning. I also enjoyed reading a lot, mainly Goosebumps and Shivers book series and the like" I explained.

"You were a Goosebumps fan too then?" She asked.

"Yep, and guess I still am!" I revealed.

"How many do you have?" She said with a smile.

"How many does William have?" I spun it the other way.

"About fifty, he's got a lot!" Amy exclaimed.

"I've got about a hundred and twenty-am not even finished!" I revealed.

Her eyes burst wide.

"What? How many is there?!" Amy exclaimed.

I thought about it, trying to work it all out in my head.

"There's 62 books in the original series alone! Then, you see, there are the multiple spin off series, Goosebumps Horrorland from one to twelve is my favourite Goosebumps spin off! I'd say about 200 altogether, and Goosebumps is STILL releasing now!" I revealed.

Her mouth dropped open.
"Wow, didn't think the books were that popular!" Amy
exclaimed. I nodded.
"He's often said to be the biggest children and teen writers
out there!" I told Amy. She nodded.
"By the way, if William wants to read any of the books he
doesn't have, I'll check my collection and lend him it if I do"
I offered. She smiled and thanked me.

We ate our dinners.
"Fancy drinking these outside?" Amy asked me, pointing to
the milkshakes. I looked outside through the window and
nodded.
"Excuse me, can we drink these on the grass please?" She
shouted to a staff member nearby.
"Yeah but we'll have to transfer it into takeaway cups. You
can't take glass outside" The staff member said. We took
our drinks to the counter and they did it for us. We went
outside.

The calm breeze felt good. We sat down on the grass and
drank our drinks.
"Erm, Amy, I don't mean to rush you, but how's it looking?" I
asked Amy, unable to stop myself. She looked at me and
smiled.
"I'm still here, aren't I?" She replied. I nodded and smiled.
"How you are feeling about William?" Amy asked.
"If he wants to and if it's okay with you...I'd be really happy
to meet him" I told the woman.

She nodded.
"Of course it's okay with me, you have to be one of the
nicest people I've ever known! I think the best way of
starting is to meet each other firstly at a fun and public

place, if William wants to. Does that sound okay with you?" Amy suggested. I thought about it and nodded.

"Now, if you really want to bring your uncle, you can. To be honest, it would probably be better to spend time with William one to one though and get to know each other" Amy explained.
"Yeah, I understand that" I replied with a smile.

"Great. Obviously, I've had to speak to my partner, William's adoptive Dad, about you and about our meeting today. I'll also have to get his say so before the meeting is arranged. I'll be certainly singing your praises though!" She told me. She paused for a minute.
"You can tell you and William are brothers!" Amy said.
"How?" I asked.
"You both blush exactly the same when someone compliments you" She said, laughing. I laughed too. I then hid my face in my hands until I felt the heat fade from it. I hate it when I blush!

"By the way, once you get to know him, if you have to torture him, please do so quietly!" Amy laughed. I laughed too but I promised that I am usually a patient, relaxed person.
We exchanged mobile numbers. She also explained she would give me the house phone number once William knew about everything.
"Does he know anything?" I enquired.
"He knows he was adopted; he found some papers my husband had left lying around on his desk three years ago. Of course, then he had a lot of questions. He took it okay and often uses it as a conversation starter! We just explained the basics, leaving out the drugs, etc. I, of course, ask you to do the same if he asks you anything, which he is bound to" Amy said.

I nodded.
"If he asks about anything, I'll just explain that I was removed from our parents when I was really young myself, so I know about as much as he does. It's partly true. My uncle only told me about the drugs part the other day, the night before I met you actually" I revealed.

She smiled and nodded.
"Your uncle as clearly done a very good job!" She said. I agreed very much so.
"Of course, I haven't met William yet, but I bet you have too!" I replied. She thanked me. At around 2p.m., we decided to part ways. I returned the cups to the café so they could be recycled, whilst Amy made sure we had not left anything before we left Canoe Lake. We walked towards her car.

"I tell you what, I'll give you a lift back home" Amy said as we neared her car.
"Thanks so much!" I showed me appreciation. She motioned for me to get in. I got into the front passenger seat.
"This isn't taking you out of your way, isn't it? I thought you lived in Southsea?" I asked her.
"I do but have to collect something from Fratton so I might as well go around and drop you off" Amy explained. I thanked her again, to which she smiled.

5

We pulled up outside my house about 15 minutes later.
"So, here you are. I'll be speaking to my husband as soon as
I see him tonight. I will message soon to arrange a meet for
you and William once I've spoken to them about it and got
their okay. William should want to meet you, he's not
exactly shy! My husbands also really nice too" Amy
explained to me.
"Thanks. Will speak to you soon!" I said. She smiled.

We said our farewells before parting ways. She drove off
with me waving. I could see her waving back. I then walked
into my house and went straight to my room. I laid on my
bed for a minute. All the excitement had suddenly worn me
out! There was a knock on my bedroom door.

"Come in!" I shouted.
Uncle Andy came strolling in. He looked down at me.
"How did it go?" He asked, checking his watch. "Is the time
a big clue?"

I smiled and nodded.
"Yeah, it went really good. She really liked me, and I do her!
Amy explained she's going to tell William about me and see
if he wants to meet me. She told me he most probably will
want to" I explained. Uncle Andy nodded.
I cleared my throat.
"Anyway, Amy also needs to talk to her husband about the

meeting too, she's assured me that he's really nice" I added. Uncle Andy smiled and gave me high five before going back to his office, leaving me to rest.

At the Jamme house, Amy was sat on her bed. She watched William play outside. Her phone rang, she answered it. It was her husband, Barry, checking how the meeting went today. After hearing it went well, Barry said that it was 'totally good with him if William and I meet'.

Later that evening, Amy sat William down on the sofa. It was getting dark outside and she had just called him in. The adoptive Mum had been thinking and planning for the talk ever since she had met me at the college. At the last minute, she decided to be more spontaneous while still being careful and sensitive.

"William, as you know, we adopted you when you were very young. I've recently found out that you have an older brother. He's 17 and I have met him a couple of times, that is where I was this afternoon. He was removed from your parents and given to his uncle, I guess he's your uncle too" Amy explained to the boy slowly and quietly.

William stared at Amy.
"Wow! Why didn't I go live with them then?" William asked. Amy nodded understandingly.
"I have spoken to Social Services about that today. They have admitted there was 'a bit' of a failure there, that you and your brother should have had contact! However, it's been decided that your uncle, who's his adoptive parent, most probably wouldn't have been granted custody of you both anyway" Amy explained to William. He nodded, taking it all in. He had so many questions roaring through his mind.

One came straight to mind...

He asked his Mum: "What's his name?".

"Freddy" Amy replied, smiling

"And is he...nice?" William asked, nervously.

"Besides you, I've never met a nicer lad. He's just so kind and very understanding. He also seems fun too!" Amy assured him. William smiled.

"Can I meet him?" William asked. Amy looked unexpectedly at William. She had not expected him to ask that quick. Although he was a confident kid, he could still be quite anxious.

Besides, who would not be in this situation.

"Erm, sure! It's entirely up to you. There's no pressure at all. Freddy's even said that" Amy told William. William looked at his feet.

"Does he want to meet me?" William asked Amy. She smiled.

"Yes, he does darling. He said he would love to" Amy told the boy. "I've now got everything I need to arrange the meeting, so it's going ahead!" Amy said with a smile, "You'll likely be meeting him at a play centre, and maybe a park afterwards for some fresh air".

William asked if he could go to his room for a bit. Amy nodded, and William walked upstairs. Amy just sat there on the sofa looking straight on at the wall in front of her. It was covered with photos.

Upstairs, William was sat at his desk doodling on the paper in front of him. As he thought more about the days ahead, a smile spread across his face.

It was now 7:20p.m. when I went to speak to my uncle in the living room.

"Hi Uncle Andy" I said. He looked towards the living room door. He had been watching T.V.

"Hey Freds, are you feeling bit more refreshed?" He asked

with a grin.

I laughed and nodded. I had obviously needed that sleep!

"Thanks Uncle Andy, for supporting me all these times and for always being there!" I told him.

My uncle gave me fist pump.

"Don't get soppy on me!" He teased. I stuck my finger out at him. He laughed.

The next day went by really fast and uneventful. I spoke more to my uncle and spoke to some friends on the phone. William also spoke to his adoptive family. One of William's neighbours had just moved out.

I was awoken by the bright sunshine pouring in through the window. I felt like a Vampire!

'I must have forgotten to close the curtains last night', I thought to myself, shaking my head. I closed the curtains for a while as I am not one for brightness when I've just woken up! It was now two days after I met Amy at Canoe Lake. I looked at the clock. The digital clock on my chest of drawers read: 08:08. Turns out I had slept very well, getting about ten hours sleep! I climbed out of bed and walked to Uncle Andy's door. It was closed but I could hear The T.V. was on so decided to leave him to it for a while.

Instead, I went downstairs for some breakfast. I heard a bump coming from the kitchen. I stopped dead in my tracks and inched forward ever so slowly. I grabbed my uncle's old golf club. I dived into the kitchen.

"Uncle Andy!" I shouted with surprise. He nearly dropped the plate of toast he was carrying.

"Freds, you made me jump!" Uncle Andy said with surprise.

"You did too!" I admitted, "I thought you was still in your room!". Uncle Andy laughed.

"Don't forget, I've got a lot of work to do today, then I'm all yours for a good week!" Uncle Andy reminded me. I nodded. "I know, don't worry about it. I'm thinking of going out today anyway" I explained. My uncle nodded and smiled.

"When I do meet William and his adoptive family, I've decided I'm not going to put in any special effort. I want to show them what I'm like on an everyday basis" I revealed to my uncle. He looked up at me.
"That sounds great. Besides, they will be more interested in your behaviour, your manners" Uncle Andy told me. I nodded.
"And I don't think you've started downing bottles of whisky recently, have you?" Uncle Andy cracked. I laughed and shook my head.
"You do know your bedroom T.V. is on, right?" I asked my uncle. He looked up then ran to turn it off.

Uncle Andy and I ate our breakfasts in silence. Me thinking about the days ahead of me. Thinking about my future. I helped my uncle to wash and dry the pots again before I went back to my room. I doodled on some paper for a bit. A short while later, I put my paper and stationary away before going into the bathroom. I started running my bath, collecting my clothes from their various locations while it was running. I shut the door.

The temperature was just right for once. I relaxed and cleaned for about half an hour before getting out and dried and dressed. I emptied the bath and picked up my pyjamas, placing them in the washing basket. Finally, I applied a tiny touch of wax into my hair.

I spent half an hour cleaning up my room a tiny bit.
I got a phone call at about 11a.m., I was tidying my room,

so I put it on loudspeaker.

"Hello?" I said.

"Hey Freddy, it's Amy" Came the reply.

"Hi Amy, how are you?" I asked.

"We are all fantastic thanks! We are off to Monkey Bizness in Gosport at around one-ish and was wondering if you wanted to meet William today? I'll pay for the taxi fare going there and I'll give you a lift back? William suggested it when I mentioned about me and him going to a soft play centre today. My husband, Barry, has to work" Amy explained. "Now, don't worry if it's too short notice, I'll just tell him that you're busy".

I thought about it and look at my digital clock.

"One this afternoon, yeah?" I clarified.

"Yeah, I know it's short notice!" Amy said apologetically.

"No, it's perfect. I haven't got any plans today anyway, was just going to go out for a bit exploring. My uncle has lots of work to do today so can't afford any distractions" I explain. "But why Gosport?" I enquire, my face creasing up.

Amy laughed.

"That'll be something we talk about during the meet" She told me.

"Cool! I'll wait for you near the reception desk!" I told her.

We exchanged farewells before I hung up.

I went downstairs and knocked on the office door. The door opened a few seconds later.

"Sorry to disturb you but I'm going out in just over an hour. I'm meeting William at Monkey Bizness at about one this afternoon. Amy's just called and invited me" I explained to my Uncle.

"Wait? The one in Gosport?" Uncle Andy asked.

I nodded and smiled.

"There's some memories for you in that place! You used to love that place, even more than the bigger and closer

ones!" He exclaimed. I laughed.
"Yeah, now I'm going there to make some memories with my brother!" I said. Uncle Andy smiled and nodded.

I told him what time I would be leaving around, and he said he would make sure he's available to see me off. I booked the taxi for 12:30p.m., so I could be sure I would be there on time to meet William. I did not want to let him down at any time, never mind before I had even met him!

6

It was an hour later. Within another hour, my life would change forever. It was the day that I would meet my little brother! As well as super excited, I was also getting nervous. I like to be responsible, but I wanted to show him that I can still be lots of fun too! I put on my Ninth Doctor t-shirt I had been wearing when I first met Amy. I had spent the time looking in my cupboards and looking through my cars, buses, vans and even more.

My uncle was sitting on the sofa, waiting for me. He motioned for me to join him. I did so.
"As you know, I'm not coming with you today, unless you really want me to?" Uncle Andy told me. I nodded.
"I should be okay thanks" I told him. Uncle Andy nodded and smiled.
"You'll be brilliant. Just be yourself and he'll love you as much as I do" He reassured me. I nodded and smiled back. I gave him a high five. I had brought a bag downstairs with me. I got a drink of water from the kitchen before I heard a horn beep. My taxi was here.

I quickly put my shoes on, grabbing the bag near the stairs.
"See you later Freds, hope you have a great time!" My uncle shouted to me as I neared the taxi. I smiled.
"Thanks! See you later Uncle Andy!" I shouted. I opened the taxi door.

"Hello Again!" The taxi driver said. It was the same one as last time! I waved to Uncle Andy as we drove off. This time he introduced himself as Shaun.
"Do you mind if I ask how the meeting went? You know, the one I took you to last time?" He asked. I laughed.

"Well, you tell me. I'm going to Monkey Bizness in Gosport to meet my little brother" I said to him. Shaun looked at me. "Well done, good for you buddy!" He congratulated me. I thanked him.

We arrived at the soft play centre in very good time. I paid Shaun the fare and a tip. He wished me luck. Thanking him, I climbed out and waved as the driver pulled the taxi out of the car park. The outside of the play centre looked smaller than I remembered from my many visits growing up.

I went into the main entrance; it was so hot outside! A young woman on the reception desk noticed me looking a bit anxious.
"Are you okay?" She asked over to me. I approached the desk.
"Oh yeah, I'm just about to meet my little brother for the first time with his adoptive Mum" I explained.
"Big day then!" She said. I nodded.
"I don't suppose I would be able to buy a small drink whilst I wait for them?" I asked. She spoke to someone else behind the desk for a moment.
"I'm afraid we don't allow that. But my manager has said that I can get you a cup of water if that's any good?" The woman said. I nodded and thanked her. She went and got me the water. I downed it and thanked her. She went to serve some customers.

I heard voices outside, I thought I could make out one of the voices. The main doors opened, revealing Amy and a boy. I recognised him from Amy's screensaver.

Amy paid for all of us at the desk and we walked through to the seating and cafe area in silence. I thought about saying something to William, but I did not know what. My mind was rattling like a bag of skittles. I had never felt anxiety like this before! We found a table on the right-hand side at the back. William made his way straight over to the play part as soon as his shoes were off. I could sense that he was just as nervous and not knowing what to say too.

"Don't worry, just go up to him. You're bound to be nervous; you are meeting for the first time" Amy encouraged me. I smiled and thanked her. I took my shoes off before walking into the play section. I found William coming off the trampolines. He then walked slowly to a quiet section of the centre. William smiled when he saw that I had chosen to follow him. He sat down.

I had not known what to say a few moments ago but I knew what to say now:
"Hey William, I'm Freddy. How are you?" I asked, sitting down in front of him.
"Hi Freddy. I'm...nervous. I've never had to do anything like this before. It's like I don't know what to say or what to do" William admitted to me, looking down at the soft floor. I nodded and looked down myself for a moment. Then I decided to be honest with him.

"You and me both. Look, there's no pressure. All we are here to do is play and lark around" I explained to the kid with a smile, motioning to the equipment around us.
"I've always tried to be brave...to not cry...or complain...or get freaked. I promised myself I wouldn't" William cried, so quiet I had trouble understanding him. I suddenly felt a wave of affection for him.
"William, I understand what you're going through. Because I'm going through it too. Everything you're feeling, I am feeling. I was shaking so much coming here, but it shows how seriously we are taking this meeting today! Although

we're just going to play on all this equipment and have fun, I'll support you through this, as we will each other" I assured him.

He looked up at me and smiled. I thought he was going to cry.
"That's why I came back here, I don't like getting freaked out in front of people...Especially places my friends could be!" William explained. I nodded.

We left the quiet section a few moments later.
"So, have you ever been here before?" William asked me.
"Yeah, I used to come here all the time growing up! I loved it!" I told him.
"Me too, I've always liked it here. It's really fun"

Amy was sat at our table. She could not believe the difference, and not just in William. I was proud of William as well as myself, the vibe felt comfortable. We played on the play equipment for about three quarters of an hour before William began to get hungry, so we went back to our table.

"I'm surprised you lasted that long without food" Amy teased him. They had arrived at the centre just over an hour ago.
"Actually, I am too a bit" I admitted. Amy laughed.
"Can we get something to eat here please, Mum? I'm really enjoying it today. I'm now so happy school was closed!" William told his Mum. William then ran to the toilet. She chuckled.

"So, how do you like William?" Amy asked me as I sat down. I smiled.
"He's great. I really like him. As we were talking, I just felt this mass of affection for him. That's when I truly knew I did so" I explained. Amy smiled.

"Can I ask what you were talking about at that moment?"
"Mostly our feelings" I answered straight away. She looked at me and nodded.
"Appears you have had quite the impact on each other. You both have got each other talking about things that you would have both considered 'forbidden' before today" Amy observed. I thought about that. I hated to admit it, but she was right.

"What do you want to do now?" She asked me.
"I'd like to get something to eat too please?" I said.
"From here?" She asked with a smile. I nodded.
Amy nodded and smiled. William came running back over.

Amy looked at him.
"Did you wash your hands properly?" She asked him.
"Yes Mum!" He said, rolling his eyes.
"Right. Have a look at the menu and decide what you both want. It's my treat this time" I insisted.
"Are you sure Freddy?" Amy asked. I nodded. Amy thanked me appreciatively, she looked at her son. William then thanked me too.
"I was ABOUT to thank him!" William insisted.

"I tell you what guys, shall we just get a quick snack here, you guys can play here a bit more? Then we'll go to a park, we'll get something bigger to eat there. We could all use a bit of fresh air!" Amy suggested.
I thought.
"Wanna go to Canoe Lake, I missed out last time?" William asked me.
"I'd love to" I said. William smiled. I could tell he was happy that I still wanted to see him more. I was happy too. I got a real good feeling that our relationship would grow into something very much like brotherhood.

We ordered some chicken nuggets and fries to share between us. We didn't really talk much whilst we ate, we were just all taking in this experience and enjoying each other's company. William and I played in the play section for another half an hour. This was a lot more tiring than I remembered!

Amy called us out. Naturally, I heard it first, I went to the front of the play section.
"Yeah, are we okay to get going? I just really want to relax in the park whilst the suns out!" Amy asked me. I smiled and nodded. I found William and brought him back to Amy.

We walked out of the building and into the vast car park ahead of us. We approached Amy's car.
"Get in wherever you want" Amy said, motioning to the car. William headed for the front passenger door.
"Erm, I mean Freddy, Mister!" Amy told William. I could tell by his face that he knew that, he was not grinning or smiling as such, more like wishful thinking on his part.
I thought and got in the back seat with William. I decided it would show William that I was fair, plus today was all about getting to know him and vice versa. Amy laughed and got into the driver's seat.

She turned to us to ensure our seatbelts were both buckled. We nodded to Amy that they were. She turned back towards the wheel and began getting ready to set off. Once she had done, William decided to start talking again.
"Do you ever miss your...our parents?" William asked. Amy spun round and looked at him.
"William! You don't ask things like that yet!" Amy scolded him.
"Erm, I didn't really know them. I went to live with my...our uncle when I was two, we're really close. He's my parent as far as I'm concerned" I explained to my brother. He nodded

and smiled.

"Sorry if that question upset you" He said quietly. I smiled and put my hand on his shoulder.

"It's natural you'd want to know more, and you didn't upset me, I'm okay concerning that topic" I told William. He smiled again; I could see the smile turning into a slight grin. I began to get 'a tad' worried.

7

"What did you look like when you were my age?" William asked, giggling. I started to reply when Amy pulled the car into Canoe Lake car park.

'Wow! That was quick!' I thought to myself. Amy turned to William with her phone out.

"See for yourself" She said, handing her son her phone.

"What?!" I gasped. I tried to grab the phone off him, but it was already too late!

William was nearly laughing. I unbuckled by seat belt and slid closer to William. He tilted the phone so I could see. How nice of him!

The photo was saved on her phone. It showed me at a sports day at my Primary School when I was around William's age. As I had told Amy before, I was quite chubby and small as a young child. William found it quite amusing. No, Wait! Now he was looking at a different photo. It was of some boy in a tutu. It fell on me like a tonne of bricks-That some boy was ME! I was around three or four and was topless and barefoot with only the tutu on!

"Where did you get these?" I asked Amy.

"The sports day one I found on your Primary School's website; I knew William might be interested in seeing a picture of you when you were his age" Amy explained.

"And what about the other one?" I asked, I was embarrassed but also actually interested.

"I friended Andy on Facebook last night and I found it on his profile" She teased. I fake laughed.

"It suits you" William said to me, giggling. I stuck my tongue out at him, to which he did one back, but added a raspberry for good measure.

Amy asked for her phone back, William handed it back to her, trying to get back to being serious again. She deleted the second photo while I watched. She asked if she could keep the first one. I reluctantly agreed since it 'didn't look that bad'.

The three of us then got out of the car and headed towards the café. This time we immediately decided to sit outside and eat. William and I both chose a toastie. Mine was ham and Cheese, William's was cheese and tomato. Amy and I turned our heads to see William running straight to the play area. Amy rolled her eyes.
"Erm, could you watch that terror please? I will go and order our stuff" She asked. I nodded and started walking towards the play area myself.
As expected, once I got to the play area, William had gotten bored and walked towards me.
"You bored already?" I asked him.
"Of the play area, yeah. I never seem to know if I wanna play until I get here" William explained.

William and I then made our way to a patch of light green grass by the lake. We sat down on the blanket; the café provides 10 giant ones dotted around the park for people having picnics!
"Don't you like tomato?" William asked me. I shook my head.
"No, I like a bit of ketchup on certain things though" I added.
"Oh, I love tomatoes!" William exclaimed immediately with a smile. I made a face.

"Is there anything you especially dislike, food and drink wise?" I asked. He thought for a moment.

"Anything weird like black pudding, haggis, pickled onions, gherkins. I do like tropical juice but don't like the individual fruits on their own" William replied.

"Is that eating the actual fruit or even the juices?"

"I think it's even juice" William exclaimed. I laughed.

"Similar to me. I love tropical juice too! I can drink the different juices individually, but I am not keen on the actual fruits" I explained. He nodded.

"What else were you like when you were around my age?" William asked me.

"Smart but rubbish at sports seems to sum me up"

"So, a bit like a geek then?"

"Not like a geek, I'm the king of geeks!" I joked. He laughed.

"I like you, your funny!" William exclaimed, giggling.

"Aren't your Mum and Dad?" I asked. He grinned but it went away almost immediately.

"Dad likes to think he is..." He said, rolling his eyes.

"I'll tell him you said that!" A voice from behind us said. We spun around. It was a woman in jogging bottoms and a dark pink T-shirt.

"You can do, he knows it" William said. I looked between them.

Amy came walking up with our drinks and food.

"Oh, Miss Rodgers! Nice to see you!" Amy said to the woman.

"You too, glad to see you're all having a great time in the great outdoors" She returned the greeting.

"Freddy, this is my teacher, Miss Rodgers. Miss Rodgers, this is my brother Freddy. I've just met him today!" William told us. I jumped up and shook her hand.

"Nice to meet you" I said to her.

"Likewise. I must wish you luck though" She joked. I laughed.
William glared at her.
She looked at her watch.
"I'll have to rush off home as am expecting something...ten
minutes ago" Miss Rodgers told us. She waved at us as she
walked very quickly towards the gates.

"Was everything okay whilst I was in the café?" Amy asked,
looking at us both. We exchanged glances and nodded.
Both me and him were still grinning a bit.
She smiled, although she could tell we were both keeping
secrets from her!
"Looks like you have a great teacher?" I observed. William
swallowed a bite of his toastie before replying.
"Yeah, Miss Rodgers is great and am really enjoying all my
classes with her!" William said.
"My tutor at college is great too-and really funny" I told him.
"What are you doing at college?" He asked.
"Computing-You know, all the normal stuff: Fixing
computers, helping to speed them up, finding out I have a
brother..." I told him. William laughed. Amy rolled her eyes.
"Don't worry, Mum does the same with Dad's jokes too!"
William cracked. I laughed.
"I actually want to sometimes, but they are often good!"
Amy told us both, she laughed.

"Hey William, Freddy's also a big Goosebumps fan and he's
got lots of cars, trucks..." Amy told her son.
"Really?" William asked with a smile.
I nodded. Then I remembered about the bag I had brought.
"Talking about cars, I've got a big collection we can share if
you want?" I offered. He thanked me cheerfully, tipping
them out onto the grass immediately with an eagerness I
recognised.

We spent an hour in Canoe Lake before we all began to feel tired.

"Err, Mum?" William asked.

"Yes?" Amy replied.

"I'm getting tired" William admitted. I looked at them.

"To be honest, I am too" I told them. Amy nodded.

"Right then, I think we'll part ways and meet up again soon if you are happy with that?" Amy suggested, looking between the two of us. William and I both exchanged glances with each other and seemed to be able to read each other's minds for that moment: Yes.

"That would be brilliant" I said.

"Yeah!" William said. Amy nodded again and stood up. We too stood up, rubbing grass and dirt off ourselves.

"I'll give you a lift back, Freddy!" Amy told me.

I smiled and nodded.

"Thanks very much, that'd be great" I said.

The three of us returned our paper plates and plastic cups before heading towards Amy's car. We got in the car, me sitting in the back again. Amy pulled us out of the car park.

"So, how have you liked today?" I asked William.

"I've enjoyed it. You're fun!" William told me.

"You too, I'm certainly not going to get bored when you're around!" I said with a laugh. William smiled. Through the front mirror, I could see Amy smile too.

We pulled up right in front of my house, around 15 minutes later.

"Thanks again Amy!" I told her. She smiled.

"No, thank you" she replied. I looked at her.

"Why?" I asked her, with a puzzled expression on my face.

"For being so nice and understanding to William. It was brilliant" Amy explained. I thought I was going to tear up, but I stopped myself.

"That's my pleasure, and I really like you both too! You are both really nice" I told them both. Amy thanked me while William nodded and smiled.

I got out of the car.
"I'd invite you in for a bit, but I know we are all tired so maybe we could do it another time?" I suggested. Amy nodded.
"Yeah, that'll be good. So, I guess we'd better get off before I end up carrying him into the house!" Amy said, motioning with her head towards the boy in the back seat.
"Yep, I'm most probably going to have a sleep for a bit too" I admitted. Amy laughed.

William slid out of the car and stood in front of me. He extended his hand to me.
"It's been great meeting you today Freddy, can we do it again very soon?" William asked, a bit nervously. I smiled, reached forward, and shook his hand. It was a great handshake for someone his age!
"Sure! I've got your Mum's number, so I'll make sure we arrange another meet up again soon" I promised William. He smiled and nodded. William got back into the car and buckled himself in. I said goodbye to them both, closed the car door and moved away from the car. I waved them off, the car honked at me and could see William waving back at me through the back window of the car. Once the car was out of sight, I walked up to my front door and used my keys to get in.

I closed the door and put my back up against it whilst I took a couple of deep breaths. I saw a set of shoes coming down the stairs. Uncle Andy appeared at the bottom of the stairs. He stopped after the last stair.

He looked at the watch I got him it for his birthday three months ago.

"How did it go?" He asked me.

"Really...Really...Well!" I replied. Excitement still filled my head so much that I found it hard to speak full sentences. Uncle Andy smiled and came a bit closer.

"What was he like?" Uncle Andy asked curiously.

"Fantastic. A 'bit' cheeky but I really lo...like him" I said.

"You were starting to say love, wasn't you?" Uncle Andy told me. I thought about it and then nodded my head.

"Why did you change it?"

"I don't feel right saying that yet. I just met him today. I do like him so much, I really do-But I can't say love" I admitted and explained. Uncle Andy nodded understandingly.

My uncle and I went into the living room, sitting down on the chairs either side of the low coffee table between us.

"We met at the reception of Monkey Bizness. We were both really nervous but once we got playing and once we had talked a bit, we had a lot of fun. We were there for just under two hours" I told him. Uncle Andy nodded.

"We then went to Canoe Lake and had some dinner" I capped off. He smiled.

"Well done Freds" My uncle said, "I'm really happy for you".

"Thanks" I said with a smile.

I told Uncle Andy I was tired so was going to have a nap. He nodded and said he was going to watch T.V. in the living room for a while. I nodded and went upstairs.

Downstairs, Uncle Andy turned on the T.V. using the remote. He did not pay any attention to it however as he took a letter off the table beside him. He held it up in front of his face and read it, obviously having read it before. He groaned quietly, and his face turned sad, he looked towards the door I had just walked out of.

8

It was now the next morning. I woke up and looked at the window. The curtains were closed allowing just slithers of light to peek round the edges. I pushed myself up into a sitting position and stretched my arms and legs. I got out of the bed and walked towards my desk. I sat down and did a few dot to dots before I got ready for college. I told Uncle Andy I'd be home for around 4p.m., before I said goodbye to him. He gave me a big hug before I ran out of the house. It is not exactly unusual for me to run late and I don't like doing so. I walked quickly along the dirt track running beside the main road, nearly slamming into a teenager obviously running late for school himself.

I entered the room.
"You're not late, Freddy" Danny told me, he was concentrating on the whiteboard in front of him. I breathed a sigh of relief. I walked up to my tutor.
"I'm sorry about running out of the college the other day. I had just found out that I have a brother" I explained.
"I know" He put the lid back on his marker. "Amy told me. We talked for a couple of minutes after you left whilst I was closing the shop up" Danny told me. I nodded.
"And no need to apologise about it. What you did was normal. You ran away from a massive change in your life. Everyone gets scared sometimes, even me, even you" Danny told me.
"Thanks Danny" I said. He nodded and I sat down. The last few of my class had just arrived so he started the class.

At Milton Park Primary School, William was in his class. He sat at a table along with four other kids. Miss Rodgers stood up from her desk.

"Right, Quieten down everyone! Let us get started!" She shouted. The room fell silent after a few seconds.

"Thanks. Now we are going to continue our work on Fractions, decimals, and percentages. Who can tell me what one twentieth is as a percentage?" Miss Rodgers asked. About Sixteen kids put their hands up.

"Yes Dominic?"

"Five percent" Dominic said.

"That's right, well done. And as a decimal?" More hands went up.

"William?"

"Yeah, zero point zero Five?" William said. Miss Rodgers smiled.

"Very good William!" Miss Rodgers congratulated him.

"How many do we need to make one whole?" Miss Rodgers continued.

A few hands went up. A member of the admin team shot into the room like The Flash and walked quickly up to the teacher. They whispered into the teacher's ear. There was a teaching assistant sat with a pupil who has special needs. "Right class, I need to run to the office to take an urgent phone call, I won't be two minutes, if you could all take a worksheet off my desk and work on them please. If you get stuck on one question, move on to the next one and I will assist you when I come back" Miss Rodgers announced. The teacher pointed to a stack of papers before she rushed out following the Admin staff member.

William walked up to get a worksheet.

"Hey William, I heard you met your brother the other day?" A voice said. He turned around to face a girl who sat at the back, she was one of the 'cool' kids, who would barely look at anyone who was not exactly like her. The whole class was now watching and listening to the two of them.

"Yeah, his name is Freddy! We met at Monkey Bizness, then we went to Canoe Lake. He's really cool" William said.
"Then, why is he even bothering with a shrimp like you?" The girl demanded.
"Because I'm his brother" William said immediately. The girl scoffed.
"Oh yeah, well, just wait until he is with his friends, he will forget all about you" The girl taunted him. William was getting visibly upset. The teaching assistant walked up and asked the girl to go back to her seat. Everyone started dispersing. William grabbed a worksheet; he could see a boy approaching.

"I'm glad you got to meet him, don't listen to her" He said, as he grabbed a worksheet before going back to his seat. The boy never spoke to any of his classmates, nothing more than mumbling if he had to anyway. William took his seat too and started working on the maths worksheet in front of him. He was usually good at maths but today, he could only just get through the easy questions. He could not get everything out of his mind.

It was now home time at William's school. He found his best friend Ben, waiting for him by the school wall. They always walked home together since Ben's family live a couple of streets away from William. They had met when Ben moved to Portsmouth in year two. Usually, Ben was as full of energy as William but today, he was leant against the wall.

William walked more quickly towards his friend.
"What's wrong?" William asked him. Ben rubbed his head.
"Nothing. Just my head is hurting" He replied. Ben stood up straight. The two began to walk home.
"How long as this been going on for?" William asked. Ben thought.

"About a month. It's nothing, everyone gets headaches, I'm fine!" Ben reassured him. William nodded.

The best friends walked in silence for a few minutes.
"Ahh!" Ben exclaimed. William looked at Ben. His friend held his head quite tightly. William saw a friend of his Mums coming towards him and flagged the car down. It pulled up beside the boys. The driver got out, leaving his hazard lights on.
"You okay guys?" He asked with concern.
"Could you give us a lift home please? My friend is not well" William asked, with a hint of worry in his voice. The guy took one look at Ben and said to wait a minute. He got back into his car and pulled it into a parking space ahead. He came back to the boys on foot.

He sat Ben down on the pavement and knelt in front of him. William sat down beside Ben.
"What's your name?" The guy asked Ben.
"Ben" He told him. The guy smiled.
"I'm Phil. I am a nurse at the local hospital. I'm friends with Amy, William's Mum" Phil explained.
"What's wrong?" Phil asked with concern and patience.
"My head hurts. Really bad" Ben admitted, his voice cracking.
"Whereabouts? Can you show me?" Phil asked.
Ben placed his hand in a couple of places on his head. It was clear to William it hurt in quite a few parts of his head. Phil nodded and smiled sympathetically.
"How long has this been going on and have there been any other problems?" Phil asked.
Ben hesitated.

"Ben?" Phil urged.
"About a month, although it started about two, three months ago, it's got really bad this month-especially this

past week. I've also been going dizzy and faint" Ben admitted to the guy.

"Right, have you actually fainted or blacked out any of those times?"

"No" Ben told him. Phil put his face in his left hand for a few seconds.

"Have you been to a doctor about this?" Phil asked Ben. Ben shook his head.

Phil then checked the time on his phone.

"I don't want to take you home, Ben. I'm afraid, I'm more fighting the urge to ring for an ambulance" Phil explained to the boy. William breathed hard a few times.

"Why, what's wrong?" William asked, his voice high.

"I don't know yet, which is why I want to do some scans sooner rather than later, to find out and help your friend" Phil assured William.

"It's just a headache!" Ben said to Phil. Phil looked down then back at the two boys in front of him.

"Chances are it is but...A few things do start off with 'just a headache'. Also, it is unusual for a headache to last this long. To your knowledge, have you ever had any conditions around your head or spine area?" Phil explained. Ben shook his head.

Phil looked at Ben and William.

"Do you have your Parent's or Guardian's number, Ben?" Phil asked. Ben told him without having to think. Phil called up Ben's Mum. He explained to her that he was taking Ben to the hospital right now to do some scans and tests. He requested them to come to the hospital.

"William, I'm afraid you can't come to the hospital with us. It is highly irregular for a nurse to carry anyone in their car, but I want to ensure Ben is okay and is seen quickly. I will keep updating your Mum and once he is out of the scans, you can come and see him" Phil explained. William nodded.

He reached over and gave Ben a hug.
"You'll be okay, you're strong" William said to Ben.
Ben thanked him before getting into Phil's car. Phil rang up
the hospital to inform them of the boy coming in.

"Will you be okay though?" Phil asked William, concerned
about his safety too.
"He'll be fine. I'll walk with him back home" A boy coming
up said. He was around Fourteen years old.
William was interested in why so nodded to Phil.
"Please...look aft..." William began.
"I will. I promise" Phil said. He jumped into the driver's seat
and made sure Ben was fastened into the passenger's seat.
Waving, they drove off towards the hospital.

William then turned towards the boy in front of him.
"Who are you? Do you know me?" William asked.
"Not yet, but I will soon. I'm Peter, I'm moving into the
house near yours in about a week" Peter explained.
"I'm William" William told Peter. They began walking home.

"What's your friend called?" Peter asked.
"Ben"
"It looks like you've known him for a while"
"Year two, so we were about six when we met. Ben was
moved up to the year above me as is seen as gifted"
William explained.
"I was seen as gifted at one point, then I woke up" Peter
joked. William laughed.
"You remind me of someone else I know" William said.
"Who?" Peter asked, looking at William.
"My brother, Freddy. I met him the other day".
"Cool" Peter said.

The two were walking on their street and stopped outside of Peter's new house. Two workers came out covered in plaster and paint.

"Hey, the house will be finished tomorrow. You'll be able to move in a couple of days!" One of them told Peter. Peter smiled.

"Thanks guys, I'll let my Mum know" Peter replied.

"Whereabouts are you stopping then?" William asked curiously.

"The trade company who's doing all the works has put us up in an hotel" Peter explained. Amy came out of her house.

"There you are, is everything okay?" She said, coming towards them.

"Yeah. I've just met our new neighbour!" William told her.

"Hi, I'm Peter, I'm moving in with my Mum" Peter introduced himself to William's Mum.

"I'm William's Mum. Call me Amy" She said.

"Your tea is on the table" Amy told her son.

William and Amy said goodbye to Peter and went inside to eat their tea. Barry came downstairs just as they sat down.

"What's for tea?" He asked his wife.

"Your favourite food" Amy replied.

"Takeaway?" He teased. Amy whacked him on the shoulder and put a plate in front of him.

"Where's my favourite!" William asked. Amy rolled her eyes.

"You had yours yesterday!" She reminded him.

9

It was now 4:30p.m. that afternoon, I was coming back from my friend's house. My phone rang. I fished my phone out of my pocket.

"Hi Freddy" Amy said.

"Oh hi, I was actually gonna ring you when I got home!" I told her.

"Oh sorry, are you okay to talk now?" Amy asked.

"Yeah, of course!" I assured her. "How are you all?"

"We're all great thanks. How are you and your uncle?

"I'm okay and Uncle Andy was okay when I rang him up at three" I explained.

"William has been bugging me to ring you and ask you when you next want to meet up" Amy admitted.

"That's why I was going to ring you when I got home as was wondering too" I informed her.

"By the way, just so you know: William's best friend that I told you about is having scans and tests as he is ill. William might, of course, seem a bit upset or distracted" Amy told me. I nodded.

"Right, no problem and I hope to help him through it, I'm sure his friend will be okay" I reassured Amy.

I was approaching my house so asked Amy to hold on whilst I unlocked the door. I went in and locked it again.

"Right. I'm in. I'll just pop and check on Uncle Andy and get my calendar loaded up on my laptop then I'll call you back about us meeting again. I'll be about ten or fifteen minutes" I suggested.

"Yes, that'll be fine. Talk to you soon".

I cut the call off and walked around the house. No one in

the living room, kitchen, office, or bedrooms. Then I looked out of the utility room window and saw my uncle in the garden. I went out and joined him.

"Hey Freds, how was Tom?" He asked, Tom is my friend I had just been to see.
"He was great thanks...and so am I" I replied. Uncle Andy smiled and laughed.
"How did College go?"
"Fine, I enjoyed it"
"Did you work in the shop or booth or whatever it is?"
"Oh no, someone else did today as there was a bit of written work I had to go over" I explained.
"Have you been okay?" I asked. He nodded.
"Yeah, good thanks" He replied.

I left my uncle to relax in the sun and went upstairs to my bedroom. I sat at my desk and started my laptop up. When it had loaded, I opened the calendar app I always use to 'book' my meetings, college days or hanging out with friends. I called Amy back.

She picked up after four rings.
"Hello?" She said.
"Hi Amy, I've got my calendar ready" I told her.
"That's good. When are you free? You would get longer on weekends, of course, but you could come around after school and college and have tea with us too if you wanted?" Amy suggested.
"How about tomorrow after school. I could walk with him from his school and stay for tea? I've got no time limits anymore" I offered.

I could hear paper flicking on the other end of the phone.
"Yeah, that sounds great to me. I'll just go and ask William if

he would like you to walk home with him from school" Amy told me. I nodded, I remembered that she cannot see me through my phone.
"Okay thanks" I said. She put me on hold for a few minutes.

Amy walked through the Jamme house to William's bedroom. She knocked on the door.
"Yeah?" William shouted. Amy opened the door. He was laid on his bed in his uniform except for his school shoes, which obviously weren't allowed on the bed.
"I'm just talking to Freddy; would you like it if he walked home with you tomorrow?" Amy asked him.
"Yeah, I'd like that!" William said immediately. Amy smiled and nodded.
"Do you want anything for pudding sweetheart?" Amy asked.
"Chocolate Pudding?"
"With Strawberry custard?"
"Yeah please Mum!"
William went back to his book whilst Amy went back downstairs and took me off hold.

"Hello?" Amy ensured I was still there.
"Hi" I said.
"Yeah, I've spoken to him and he's very happy that you are meeting him after school" Amy admitted.
"What time?" I asked.
"Err, School finishes at 3:15p.m. so if you get there for that time, you'll be there on time. He usually meets his friend against the school wall so I'm guessing that's where he'll want to meet you" Amy explained.
"Okay, no problem" I said.
I put it in my calendar and set an alarm on my phone, so I would set off in time to be at William's school for 3:15p.m.

"Great, any idea what you might want for tea?"

"I'll just have whatever you guys having please" I said.

"I was thinking of doing spaghetti Bolognese tomorrow" Amy suggested.

"That would be brilliant thanks!" I showed my appreciation.

"No problem at all! I'll let you get off as I'm going to make us some pudding now. I'll see you both around 3:35p.m. If he wants to go to the local park, it's alright, just ring me and let me know so I'm not wondering where you both are" Amy requested.

"Will do and yep, I'll see you tomorrow! Looking forward to it" I said.

"Me too! See you tomorrow" She replied, before cutting off. I put the phone down and made sure the event was saved in my calendar and my phone.

At the Jamme household, the house phone rang. It was now 7p.m; Barry answered the phone in the kitchen. Amy was tidying the living room. William was having a bath and listening to a joke C.D., he could be heard laughing. Barry nodded his head every few seconds and kept saying "Right", "Okay", "Yes" or "No".

"When do you want us to tell him?" Barry asked the caller. There was a couple of minutes silence whilst the caller spoke. He sighed and looked upstairs. He then quickly looked back at the wall.

"Mmm....Well, of course I'll respect his wishes and hope he is not feeling too bad"

"Your welcome and I am really sorry" Barry said. They exchanged farewells and Barry put the phone down slowly.

<u>*10*</u>

It was the next day, a shutter breakdown on the booth meant it had to be closed today. I spent all day in the classroom apart from ten minutes whilst getting a sandwich. Danny came in whilst I was eating. He sat down at the head of the table; I was sitting two seats on his left. I had not even looked up.
"Freddy, What's wrong?" He asked.
"Nothing, I'm fine" I mumbled.
"Is that Finnish for 'I'm not fine but I will put on a seemingly see-through face'?" Danny said.

I looked up at him.
"You know, I get that look all the time off my grandson and nephew, not to mention a lot of the student's I've had over the years. You get used to that face" Danny explained.
I kept looking down at the table, eating my sandwich.
"Freddy, something is bothering you, please just tell me what it is? That's another part of my job as your tutor. Please, trust me" Danny said.

I took a deep breath and swallowed, although I had nothing in my mouth.
"Don't want to mess up" I said quietly after a minute.
"Mess what up?" He asked understandingly.
"I'm meeting with William after school" I told my tutor, pulling myself together a bit.
"William's your brother, right? Are you staying there for tea too?" Danny asked me.

I nodded.
"Yeah. He's great. I don't want to mess it up or make him hate me" I admitted. I looked down at the table again.

"How can you mess it up? How can you make him HATE you? You are not thinking rationally. You are scared! Scared about things which most probably won't happen" Danny told me.
"I've not been around for all of his ten years before now and suddenly, it's like I'm barging into his life. I want him to like me" I explained.

"It was Social Services who failed you both. You missed out too Freddy, missed out on a little brother for TEN years. You need to find a way to put this aside, otherwise...otherwise it WILL go wrong and although I'm sure he still wouldn't hate you; he'll likely become more nervous around you". Danny started,
"You didn't barge into his life, your lives are colliding, your worlds. He agreed to meet you and I'm sure he was excited about it; I know his Mum was! You are a great, caring, and compassionate person, Freddy. Accept that for once in your life" Danny told me.
"How do I do that? I can't get it out of my mind!" I asked.
"With help and support from those around you" He said instantly. I looked up at him.
"Let us help you" Danny asked me. I nodded slowly.

"Now, I'm very happy about your college work, in fact you're in front of most in the group. Your task for this afternoon whilst everyone else catches up is: Ways you and William can feel more comfortable communicating" Danny instructed me.

"I've thought about writing down the things we could talk about?" I told my tutor. Danny nodded and smiled.
"A guideline of what you could talk about could be a great idea, like a list of subject matters. Just, don't make it into a 'script', as you can always tell when it is pre-planned and it's better when speech is spontaneous. More fun and

accepting!" Danny warned me. I nodded.
"Okay, I'll try" I agreed.
"That's all we can do" Danny told me quietly. He stood up and walked towards his office in silence. I carried on eating my sandwich.

It was lunchtime at William's school. He was outside in the playground. He was watching the girls' football practice. A girl spotted him. Annabel. The girl who had picked on him the day before.
"Who are you looking at, Shrimp?" She shouted. He looked down. He heard advancing footsteps which made him look up. Annabel was stood right in front of him looking down on him.

He stood up.
"What do you want?" William asked.
"To see how you like it" She said, coldly staring at him.
"I'm allowed to watch a game of football" William defended himself, "My friend I'm usually with at breaks is away".
"Away, you mean in hospital? Guessing you haven't heard then?"
"Heard what?!" William asked, worriedly.
"Ask your 'family'" Annabel whispered, before running back to the field. William had had enough, he walked back towards the pupil entrance and asked to be let in early. The deputy headteacher told him to go straight to the library.

The rest of the afternoon ran pretty uneventfully. Annabel was at the local football stadium on a visit with the others in the football club. William was glad for the peace. Someone else picked on the quiet boy and William invited him to sit next to him as the kid who usually sat next to William was off ill. The boy's teaching assistant joined them too.

The classroom clock read: 2:40p.m. Danny said I could leave now to make sure that I would be there in time.

"Remember, focus on the present. Believe in yourself, believe in him" Danny said to me. I smiled before walking to the school. It was a long walk, about half an hour. I reached the primary school around five minutes before school finished so I got me and William a Slushie each.

A girl advanced.

"Who are you? Have you been held back for the last ten years?" She cracked, cruelly.

"No, I'm here to pick someone up" I explained.

"Who?" She asked.

"William, William Jamme" I told her.

"Oh right, the brother who's not been around for ten years. What a role model you are" She said.

"That was not by choice, I can assure you. Me nor my uncle were told I had a brother. It's upset me a lot" I corrected her.

"I shouldn't tell you this but...I spoke to William at lunchtime and he mentioned you. I don't think he has the guts to tell you, but he doesn't like you much, he's worried about his family around you" The girl told Freddy. A woman shouted for the girl and she took off running.

The doors opened, and all the kids and staff came pouring out. William came out looking around, he grinned when he saw me.

"Hi" I said.

"Hi Freddy, how are you?" He asked.

"Fine thanks" I said. He stared at me oddly as we turned off the path and on to a cycle track with bushes on either end.

"This wasn't the brother I met…" William cried. I looked down.
"There's an explanation for that" A voice said behind us. It was the teen I had bumped into on the way to college that day.
"Hi Peter" William said, sounding very upset.

"Freddy, I'm guessing? Just tell him what happened!" Peter told me, looking between the two of us. William was looking down at his shoes; I thought I could see a few tears in his eyes. I took a deep breath. The path had benches dotted along it and led my brother and Peter to one. I sat down. William sat down too.
"Your friend or classmate came up to me, just before you came out. She told me what you think. That you're scared of me…" I told him.

William looked up at me with wet eyes.
"What? I've never said that, I…" William started then hesitated.
"This might be a good time for you to be open too" Peter told William.
"I am not scared of you, the complete opposite. I want to do more with you, it's Mum that's saying no to the ideas. It's only stuff like rock climbing, cinema and bowling" William explained. His eyes were still wet, but he had stopped tearing up.

"Who was this person, the one who told you all of this?" William asked me.
"I don't know. It was a girl around your age, reddish hair…" I began. William's eyes shot open. He interrupted me.
"Her name was Annabel, wasn't it?" William asked.
"Yeah?".
"Nothing she says is true. She's an idiot from my class.

Nothing to worry about, she just talks tough. Annabel picks on everyone who isn't like her" William admitted.

Peter spoke up:
"I'm going to walk on ahead and leave you both to it" He said, speed walking towards his house. He waved to us as he did.

"How could you believe her after the great time we had when we met? Didn't you enjoy it?" William asked, looking hurt. I took a breath.
"It was the best day of my life; one I'll never forget. I met my brother. I shouldn't have believed something a girl I didn't even know had said" I told him.
"Then why did you?" My brother asked me.
I stayed silent for a minute.
"Because I'm scared. Ever since I found out about you".
"Scared of what?" William asked, confused. I turned to look at William.
"Of me messing up. I want you to think I'm a good brother and I can't get the fact out of my head that..." I started,
"How can I be a good brother to you when I haven't been there for ten years" I admitted.

"How was you to know?" William asked. "We could all blame ourselves and the people around us. My Mum and your...our uncle could have enquired if we had brothers or Sisters at any point, Social Services should have arranged for us to meet much sooner. The point is...".
"That we're here now" I finished his sentence. William smiled. I thought for a moment in the silence.
"When we get in, why don't I have a word with Amy about doing some of things you have suggested?" I offered. He smiled cheerfully.
"Great! I wonder why she was putting it off?" William asked.

I thought about it for a minute.

"I know Amy, she's great and kind. There will be reasons why she believes it isn't for the best, which is what I've got to find out as well. It could be..." I started.

"What?" William asked with eagerness.

"What she could be thinking is: Doing lots of activities like that might give us false hope that we'll become 'perfect' brothers" I thought out loud. William looked at me.

"But you understand that we will still have disagreements at times like we have just done, and that's normal with family?" I asked him. He nodded.

"Yeah I do" William said. I smiled. I put my arm around his shoulders.

"Thanks for talking to me" I told him.

"Oh god, don't get soppy!" He cried, half-jokingly. He shoved my head. I laughed and gave his head a small shove back.

I sent Amy a text to confirm that we were okay and had just sat down for a few minutes. We stood up and began walking home again.

We were walking up to William's house when we saw a removal van outside a house nearby. Peter came out of the house.

"Hi guys, how's it going?" He asked.

"Great thanks. You're finally moving in then?" William figured.

"How did you guess?" I teased him

"Well, the removal tru..." He started. I rolled my eyes.

"Oh, shut up!" I said. Peter laughed.

A woman carrying a box came walking towards the house.

"Mum, this lad is our new neighbour I met the other day"

Peter told her, pointing to William. She put the box on the floor.

"Oh cool, I'm Peter's Mum..." She started.

"In case me calling her 'Mum' didn't give you a clue" Peter cracked. We both laughed.

"It's a shame that you're not that enthusiastic at helping your poor Mum with the boxes!" She said to her son.

"Okay, which boxes do you want me to move?" Peter said, unwillingly. She pointed to two boxes.

"Sorry about that, you can call me Sally" Peter's mum told William and me.

"I'm Freddy, I'm William's brother" I introduced himself.

"With you saying that, I can see some similarities" She observed.

We nodded and said we should get home, explaining we were late anyway!

"No problem, speak to you later guys!" Sally said. Peter waved. We waved back.

With William in front, we entered the house.

"Hello, it's only us!" I shouted in. William made his way to the kitchen, he motioned for me to follow him. A man was at the cupboard top with his back to us.

"Hi Dad" William greeted him. I gasped and nearly jumped back when he turned around.

11

"What's wrong?" William's Dad asked with concern. I laughed.
"Sorry, you look just like Harrison Wells from The Flash!" I told him. William burst out laughing.
"So, I've been told...repeatedly!" He told me. I nodded.
"I'm Barry. Great to finally meet you, Freddy. William and Amy have spoken very much and greatly of you, especially William. He never stops going on about you!" Barry told me, with a smirk.
"Dad!!!" William said, his face turning red. I laughed.
"Thanks very much and it's nice to finally meet you too!" I returned the greeting. William's face was finally returning to its peachy colour. Footsteps came down the stairs.

"Oh, hi Freddy!" Amy greeted me, coming into the kitchen.
"What about me?!" William said.
"Hello to you too William" Amy said to him.
"I'll put tea on in a little bit. You can play or something if you want?" Amy offered. William nodded and dragged me to the stairs.

William opened the door to his room. It was painted yellow and blue with bits of white. I thought it was very cool. William went over to a tall, wooden, built in cupboard to one side of his room. He disappeared into it. I went towards it after a minute, wondering where he had gone.

Right at the back was a secret crawlspace which led to a stone room. William was knelt on a rug picking up cars and vans.

"What is this place?" I asked, looking around in wonder. William looked at me then he came and stood beside me. "This is my space. A room which allows me to relax and to have complete privacy. No one knows about this...No one but you" William explained.

"You did this?" I asked, looking around.
"I noticed the piece of board at the back of the cupboard about three years ago. I took it off, just to see what was on the other end. When I found this room, I was in my dreams!" William explained.
I nodded.
"I will keep this a secret, under one condition: You can promise me that you're safe at all times whilst in here?" I said. He nodded.
"Yeah, I'm safe in here. Trust me, I checked everything out when I first found it!" William assured me. I nodded. We left the cupboard and entered William's room.

"Want to play Buzz?" William asked.
"What's that?" I asked him.
"It's a quiz game I have on my PlayStation Two, it's really cool!" William said. He set everything up whilst I untangled the buzzers that you play the game with.
He then turned it on, and we were going through the options.

We got up to the buzzer sounds.
"I like to do this!" William said. He kept his thumb pressed down on the yellow button at the bottom of the buzzer. The different sounds all played at once. There was sounds of dogs, cats, trains, stadiums, and frogs among many others. I joined in with him, but I held down my blue button. William laughed at the racket we made. We only did that for twenty seconds before I told him to stop it before we really peed

his Mum or Dad off! He agreed, and we proceeded to the actual game.

It was called the Big Quiz, so the questions had a bit of everything. The game was about 15 years old, so a lot of the music and stuff was released years before William was born and I was only an infant myself. Still, we both did well. Our guesses were educated, and I beat him by just over ten points. We had really good fun and learnt a lot too.

Amy came into the room. The door was open.
"Hi guys, you having fun?" She asked. We both nodded.
"Me and Barry will challenge you after tea if you want?" Amy offered. William and I exchanged glances and nodded.
"Great! Well, tea's ready!" She told us. We followed Amy downstairs.
We went down and had our tea. As she had suggested last night, we had Spaghetti Bolognese. Amy is a great cook!

"Now, I have received the phone call and it's okay for Ben to have visitors" Barry told his son. William looked at him thoughtfully.
"If you want to go, go!" I encouraged him. "I can always come here another time".
"I want him to meet you, if that's okay?" My Brother said.
"Sure! Who is this Ben?" I enquired.
"My best friend" William replied.
"Capital 'B'. They met years ago and have been inseparable ever since. He's William's age but got moved up to the year above as is very smart" Amy explained to me.
"Aren't I?" William asked. Amy rolled her eyes.
"Yes, you are sweetheart" Amy told him.
"And we're not THAT close!" William corrected her.
"Oh really?" Barry interrupted. "Shall we talk about the glue thing?".

"No!!" William shouted. I could tell whatever had happened was embarrassing.

"Right, getting serious, do you want me to drive you to the Hospital or do you want to leave it till tomorrow?" Amy asked William.
"I want to go today" William said immediately.
"And you want me to come?" I asked again.
"Yeah" He answered. The parents nodded at each other. We finished our teas before putting our coats and shoes on. Barry stayed at the house to do some housework whilst Amy took William and me to the hospital.

We walked down the long corridor. The drive had taken around fifteen minutes and could tell my brother was getting eager to see his friend. We waited at the reception and told them who we were here to see. We were pointed in the direction of his room.

Amy knocked on the door.
"Come in" A male voice answered. Amy and William both recognised it so went in with Amy leading.
"You've got a visitor!" Amy told Ben.
"Hi William!" Ben said.
"Hi, how are you doing Ben?" William asked.
"Not too bad, the Morphine, paracetamol and Codeine they're pumping into me is helping me fight the pain" Ben told him.
"That's good. This is my brother, Freddy. Freddy, this is Ben, you've heard how close we are" William introduced us.
"Hi" Ben and I said at the same time.

About five minutes later, the man stood up.
"Wanna get some Coffee?" The man asked Amy.
"You do know me then! I'm surprised you had to ask" Amy

joked. The guy chuckled.

"By the way, Freddy, this is my friend Phil. I've known him since before William came into my life" Amy informed me.

"Good to meet you!" Phil said cheerfully before leading Amy out towards the hospital canteen.

That left Ben, William, and me in the room. After a few minutes of talking:

"I'm bored!" Ben exclaimed.

"Me too" William admitted. I felt something in my pocket. I pulled it out.

"Hey guys, I've got these in my pocket. I don't know how your cards got in my pocket though!" I told William. He shrugged.

"It's no problem. We were packing stuff away at home before tea" William reminded me.

"You must have put them in your pocket, so you could carry more and forgot they were in there" Ben suggested. I nodded.

"Amy and William said you were smart" I told him.

He smiled.

"Look where it's gotten me though" Ben said, his smile soon fading away.

"Hey, you're are going to be okay Ben! That's why you are here" I assured him.

"Thanks" Ben replied. I nodded. We spent 20 minutes playing card games before Phil and Amy got back.

"What took so long?" William asked with interest.

"Phil offered me a coffee, so naturally I had two. We sat with Ben's parents, so we were talking too" Amy told us. I laughed; Ben and William rolled their eyes.

"You boys being having fun?" Amy asked, spotting the cards on the hospital bed.

"Yeah, it's been great!" Ben said. William and I agreed.

"Well, visiting times just about over guys. You might want to think about saying your goodbyes and getting ready for when they ring their bell" Phil suggested.
"Err...Freddy..." Ben asked.
"Yeah?".
"Can I talk to you in private for a moment, if that's okay Phil?" Ben asked. I could tell he was nervous about asking me for this, he had only just met me after all! Phil nodded that it would be okay.

"Okay, we'll wait for you at the car then Freddy" Amy said. I nodded and smiled.
"I'll come and see you again really soon!" William told Ben.
"I can't wait!" Ben said with a light smile.
"Bye Ben!" William said. Ben returned the farewell before William walked out of the room.
"Goodbye Ben" Amy said, Ben waved back. She exited the room with Phil.

12

"What's up?" I asked Ben. He took a deep breath.

"Promise...William will not know..." Ben said.

"I promise" I said.

"I'm not going to get better" Ben told me, "I'm going to keep getting worse. I won't be leaving the hospital". I sighed.

"So, you mean..." I started.

"I've been given about a month to live" Ben said.

"I'm really sorry! I can't imagine how it feels to know that" I said, looking at him with sympathy.

"It's okay. I'm prepared" Ben told me, with a smile.

"So, I take it that William doesn't know?" I guessed. He shook his head.

"His Mum and Dad do but not William-And he mustn't know!" Ben told me.

"How come?".

"I just don't want him to know..." He told me. I breathed a deep breath and nodded.

"If Amy and Barry have agreed to keep it a secret, so will I. But it must be noted that I don't think this is the best way to go about this" I admitted to Ben.

"I know. You don't think everyone doesn't think the same, do you? I don't want it to get weird between William and me. If he finds out, we'll get all mushy and emotional and I want one relationship that's fully familiar" Ben explained to me. I nodded understandably.

"Now, what was this sticking thing Barry hinted about?" I asked Ben.

"Huh?".

"He said something about a sticking incident between you

and William?" I explained.

"Basically, when we were in year four and three respectfully, our classes were put together for a week and we were put into pairs. William and I were paired with each other for obvious reasons. We were given a different task on each day. On the third day, we used too much glue, we had both been putting glue on without realizing. We touched the thing we were making, and William decided to put his hands on my shoulders 'in order to try and shake some sense into me' and became stuck. I tried to get us unstuck, but then I became stuck to him too" Ben explained.

"I can see how embarrassing that would have been" I observed. Ben laughed.
"It kind of was...but due to how confident we both are, it was okay" Ben told me.
"I know we've only just met but if you ever want to talk, I'm here" I told him, giving him a piece of paper with my number on.
"Thanks Freddy" Ben said, looking at the slip in his hands.

There was a knock on the door.
"Come in" Ben shouted.
Phil came in.
"Are you finished?".
Ben and I exchanged glances and nodded.
"Well, once you've said your goodbyes, I'll escort you out of the children's ward" Phil told me. I nodded.
"See you soon!" Ben said.
"You certainly will. Remember everything we talked about and how you've got my number" I reminded him. Ben smiled and nodded. Phil then walked me out of the room.

About three minutes later, I was walking down an empty,

dimly lit corridor.

I got into the car; William looked at me as I fastened myself in.
"All sorted?" Amy asked. I nodded.
"What do you think?" William asked me.
"I think you've found the best friend" I told him, smiling. I could not get it out of my mind what was happening. I was not even sure that I was doing the right thing, the right thing for William.
"Right, William's admitted to me that he's got loads of homework to do so do you want to come by tomorrow or another afternoon?" Amy asked.

I thought.
"Want any help with it?" I asked William. "That's if that's okay with you?". Amy smiled and nodded.
"Yeah please" William admitted.
"What type is it?" I enquired. Perhaps I should have started off with that!
"Geography and Maths, I think" William told me. I nodded. I was really good at Maths, not so good at Geography! However, I knew I should at least try and help my brother with it. Plus, it would not exactly be cheating to do some research.

I woke up the following morning, this being my day off college. I went and visited my other friend and played some games with him. My uncle had been busy doing housework when I had left but was now sat on an armchair in the living room.

He picked up the house phone. The volume was up loud, and the voice could be heard faintly talking back to him.
"Hello?" The voice said on the other end.

"Hi Amy, it's Andy Lewis" My uncle said.

"Oh, hi Andy! Nice to hear from you! What can I do for you?" Amy asked.

"I need to talk to you about something, in person" Uncle Andy told her.

"Oh okay, well, it would be great to meet you! When would you like to do this?".

"As soon as possible. It's not an emergency but I feel it is quite urgent" Uncle Andy admitted.

"No problem. I'll be free in about an hour if that's any good? I can come to yours?" Amy suggested.

"That would be great thanks. Just one thing, can you keep this quiet from Freddy please? It's kind of about him" Uncle Andy asked.

"Erm, sure! I do need to ask though: Is there anything up with Freddy?" Amy asked with concern.

"No, it's just a...complication" Uncle Andy answered.

They said farewell to each other before they cut the call off. Uncle Andy held the phone in his hands and stared straight ahead.

Amy met my uncle outside of my house. She looked clueless as to what this could be about, much less how serious it was. Uncle Andy invited her in. They talked for about 20 minutes, the voices were inaudible, but their expressions showed that whatever the issue was-It was not good. Was not good at all!

13

I was walking back from my friend's house. I heard kids up ahead. They were laughing, talking, shouting. It took me a couple of seconds for me to remember the school and the fact it had just become home time. It was the school which my brother attends. As I walked along the school fence, I happened to turn my eye slightly back to the school. Then I saw four kids on top of William and another kid.

I shouted and ran towards them, the culprits dispersed quickly. The two boys were fighting for their breaths.
"What the hell was that?" I asked them.
"Two of those kids were picking on him and I went over to help him, and they called their friends over" William explained. I looked for the kids.

A teacher advanced.
"Who are you please?" He asked me. Another teacher came running up. I had met her at the park during our first meeting. Miss Rodgers.
"He's William's brother" She told the other teacher. "Nice to see you again Freddy!".
I nodded.
"Is there a problem?" The first teacher asked.
"Erm yeah, I've just stopped four kids in the middle of beating up William and his friend" I told them.
"Right, I'm sorry to hear that!" Miss Rodgers said.
"Can any of you identify the kids or any reason they might have targeted you? The other teacher asked us.

I looked at William.
"Two kids were picking on Kaleb and when I went over to help him, their friends came over and started taunting us

and beating us" William explained.

"Freddy, can you walk with me home please?" William asked, nervously. I smiled and nodded.
"What about your friend?" I asked.
"His Dad usually comes and picks him up in his car" My brother told me. I nodded.
"Right. A lot of kids have already left; can you see any of the ones who attacked you?" Miss Rodgers asked the two boys. They looked around.
"No, they're gone" William said. Kaleb just shook his head. Miss Rodgers and the other teacher looked at me.
"No, they are not here. They legged it and scattered as soon as I came running over" I informed them.

"Right to stop this getting messy and complicated, can you write us a statement on what happened guys?" The other teacher asked. "You too Freddy, on what you saw and what you did?".

We all exchanged glances. I could tell that both boys, especially Kaleb were very shaken.
"Erm, I think the boys need to have some space first before they write theirs. I'm more than willing to come in first thing tomorrow with William?" I offered. William smiled.
Miss Rodgers and the other teacher exchanged glances. I could tell the other teacher was against it, but Miss Rodgers flashed us a warm and understanding smile.
"Of course, I fully understand. Just do us a big favour before you go: Do you know any of their names?" She asked.

The two boys thought.
"Annabel from my class, Jamie Dunn from year six, Chris from my class, I don't know the fourth person" William reeled off. I could tell Kaleb wanted to say something, so I

hovered my finger near his lips and pointed to my ear. He looked at me. Kaleb then drew his mouth to my ear and whispered a name very quietly:

"David Stockle".

"Stockle?" I whispered. He nodded.

"Yeah, the last kid was David Stockle" I told the teachers.

"From year six?" Miss Rodgers asked Kaleb in a patient manner. He nodded slowly.

"Right, we'll keep a strong eye on them in morning to ensure you and others are safe" The other teacher, whose badge read: Mr Quent told us. William and I nodded and thanked him.

"So, do you want all of us to come in tomorrow then to give a statement? I enquired.

"Yes please, all of you. You can come in together if you want. This includes if you wanted to come in after we have the accused kids in our line of sight?" Mr Quent suggested.

I looked at Kaleb. He nodded at me, so did William.

"Great, so just come to the school for about nine-ish tomorrow morning and speak to the Headmistress, Ms Fowler, she's really nice" Miss Rodgers reassured us. We all nodded and agreed to do that. I rang the college to notify them that I would be in late tomorrow. As soon as I cut off, Kaleb's Dad arrived to pick him up. He ran for the car and dived in. The car went on up the road.

William and I said farewell to the teachers before departing to William's house. We walked via the cycle track again. We walked mostly in silence but also had some laughs too.

I got a text from my uncle: 'Hi Freds, can I please speak to you at the house please, It's not urgent".

"Erm William, Uncle Andy wants to see me so will you be

okay if I drop you off at home and will pick you up from your house tomorrow and walk to the school with you?" I asked my brother. He looked at me and nodded.

"I'm sorry I'm putting you through this" William said. I stopped and held William in place.

"Hey, you don't need to apologise! This is certainly not YOUR fault. You are the bravest kid I have had the honour of knowing. I'm so proud of you for helping the other boy!" I told him. He smiled, a real smile too. Unexpectedly, he gave me a hug, I put my arms around his shoulders. The first hug between us.

I dropped my brother off at his house and explained the basics to Barry and told him I would walk with William to School tomorrow. Amy was out. Barry thanked me for looking after his son. I nodded and smiled before exiting.

As I was walking up the street, a car pulled up beside me: Amy.

"Hey Freddy, are you going to Andy's? If so, do you want a lift?" She asked.

"Err, yeah please!" I said appreciatively. She smiled and said to get in. I got in the front passenger seat this time. She drove in silence; I could tell something was on her mind.

"You okay?" I asked her. She turned her head and smiled at me. This smile was exaggerated.

"I am thanks. What about you?" She asked. I nodded and said I was good.

She pulled up outside my home.

"Freddy, I just want to say: I'm always here for you- Remember that!" Amy told me. I smiled and thanked her. I got out and waved her off. I walked into my house.

14

I found Uncle Andy in the living room.
"Hi Freds, can you sit down a minute. I need to talk to you"
Uncle Andy told me, sounding serious and emotional. I
could tell this talk was going to be hard.
"Until a year before your parents had you, I lived in the
Czech Republic for ten years. I had a wife and everything.
We broke up a month before I moved back to the U.K.
Anyway, we had frozen my... 'essence' and she got pregnant
with our twins six years ago" He started.

"Okay?" I said. I did not understand where this was going.
"Freds...She's dying and there's no one to look after the
kids" Uncle Andy informed me.
"You mean?" I guessed.
"Yeah, I have to move back to the Czech Republic to look
after the kids. There is one boy and one girl. They're right
little terrors apparently!" He told me, with a little laugh.
"But...I've got my brother here now?" I reminded Uncle
Andy. He nodded.
"I know, that's why...That's why I don't want you to come
with me" Uncle Andy told me.

I breathed hard.
"YOUR new chapter has already started, and it can't be
allowed to finish" Uncle Andy told me.
I looked up at him.
"You know what, you've looked after me for fourteen Years
when I needed you the most. Now those Five-year olds
need you. Just promise me one thing..." I told my uncle.

He smiled a sad smile.
"Anything, Freds" He said.

"That I'll see you still" I asked, with loads of questions and emotions roaring through my mind. Uncle Andy smiled.
"Of course, you will. You can come and visit me in the Czech Republic, and you know, the kids would love Hampshire!" Uncle Andy said, with a smile. I nodded with a smile too. He reached over and gave me a hug.

"However, you are still and always will be my number one priority! Therefore, I have spoken to Amy. I'd like you to move in with Amy, William, and Barry. At least until you are ready to live alone" Uncle Andy told me. I thought and nodded.
"Are William and I ready for that?" I asked. He smiled.
"Are you kidding me? I haven't been around the two of you, but Amy told me that the bond between you two is amazing! And you'll still have minor disagreements and that's normal, no matter how long you've known each other" Uncle Andy told me. I smiled. He was right.
"I love him" I admitted to my uncle.

He looked up at me and grinned.
"Hey, well done!" Uncle Andy said to me.
"We even hugged this afternoon; I'm helping him sort this complication out at school" I told my uncle. He smiled.
"Nice job" He said. I nodded. I asked if I could go upstairs and take it all in properly. Uncle Andy nodded and motioned with his hand understandingly. I walked upstairs to my room and lied on my bed.

"William, can I speak to you for a minute please!" Amy shouted upstairs in the Jamme house.
William came out of his room.
"What's wrong, Mum?" He asked his Mum. He thought it was about what happened at school. Deep down, he really wanted to face it with me or at least his Dad, his Mum could

often get soppy and overprotective.
"I just need to talk to you about something that's happening in the near future" Amy told William.

William joined Barry and Amy. He sat in the soft chair in front of his adoptive parents.
"Your Uncle Andy, Freddy's adoptive parent, is having to move abroad to look after his other kids" Amy started.
"How long for?".
"For good, their Mum is not going to be in a fit state to look after them".
"So, he's moving away for good?" William asked.
"Yes darling" Amy said. He suddenly ran upstairs, shutting the living room door to slow his parents down.

Amy and Barry ran up after him. William locked his bedroom door so they would have to get the key. Barry ran to his and Amy's bedroom to collect the key. He unlocked the door and found the bedroom window open. It was a fire escape and the equipment to get out was activated.

They ran around the house and searched everywhere. They then checked their street. No sign of the boy. Amy then did the first thing that came into her head.
"Hi Freddy, it's Amy" She said.
"Hi Amy, I'm not really in the mood for talking right now..." I said, about to put the phone down.
"No! William's ran away!" Amy shouted. That sent a jolt through me and made me put the phone up to my ear again.
"What?".
"He's ran away from the house, just now" Amy told me again. I said I would be there as soon as possible.

I told my uncle I was going to see William. I started running up the street. It was a long way. I saw a familiar looking car coming towards me. A taxi. I flagged it down.

"Hey mate, you okay?" The taxi driver asked.

It was Shaun.

"No, my brother's ran away" I told him. His eyes flashed with worry. He told me to get in. I did so. He turned his taxi system off.

"Maybe Canoe Lake?" He suggested. I thought and nodded. I rang Amy back up and kept talking to her. We pulled into Canoe Lake car park. Shaun and I then searched the whole park. We spoke to the staff in the café and showed them pictures, two of them remembered him from the day the two of us first met! We checked Monkey Bizness in Gosport where we had first met. The staff there remembered us but had not seen William since that day.

William was not found in Canoe Lake or Monkey Bizness. Amy and Barry searched their local park, the cycle track, and the streets nearby. Nothing. Shaun drove me to their house. Shaun then said he would drive back to canoe Lake and update us if anything came about. I thanked him, Amy came out and thanked him too. Barry was on the phone to some of William's friends' parents, hoping he had just run to one of them to cool off. Amy led me into the house. Barry got off the phone as we walked into the house.

"I don't get it?" Barry blurted out as we walked through the house again.

"Get what?" I asked.

"We should have seen him" Barry said.

"What do you mean?".

"Well, he darted out of the bedroom window" Amy told me.

"So?" I asked.

"We were right behind him" Barry informed me. I

remembered that his bedroom window was a fire escape, with steps attached to the wall, either side, activated by a switch beside the steps on this side. He still must have been fast! Memories flickered back, then I remembered.

"I've found him" I declared.

"How?!" Amy asked.
"I...I can't tell you. Please, for the sake of our future relationship, please leave this to me" I asked them. They exchanged glances.
"What do you need us to do?" Amy asked.
"Not to open William's bedroom door" I asked.
"We already checked his bedroom. Under his bed, his cupboards and everything" Barry informed me.
"Please...just trust me" I pleaded. They looked me in the eyes and went downstairs. I took a deep breath. I walked into his bedroom. I closed the door behind me and went straight up to his cupboard. I opened it and slipped into the crawl space. I climbed into the stone room and there he was. I fastened the wall back shut.

"Hey" I said. He spun around slowly.
"What are you doing here?" He asked me.
"You went missing, where else would I be" I replied.
"Why do you care? You're leaving my life anyway" William muttered.
"I care about you" I said, getting emotional.
"Then why are you leaving me?" He cried.
"I'm not leaving you! I'm coming to live with you!" I shouted, all of a sudden.

"What?" William asked quietly. I took a breath.
"Uncle Andy is moving back to Czech Republic to take care of his other kids. Amy, Barry and Uncle Andy have decided

that I should live here" I explained to William.
"And what do you think?" William asked me.

"What do you think?" I asked him. "Honestly!".
"I really want you to" He admitted.
"So do I" I told him.
"Then why did you hesitate each time I asked?" William shouted.
"It is another change!" I shouted.

"It is yet another change in a very short amount of time with little time to take it in or to think" I said with a raised voice, but not shouting now.
"What is there to think about?" William asked.
"This is gonna be a big change, and not just for me!" I warned him.

"How?!" He demanded.
"Count the number of bedrooms in this house" I told him. I could see his eyes searching the house.
"Among lots of other changes, you'd likely need to share a room with me" I informed him. I saw his eyes light up.
"I'd like that? That would be fun!" William admitted.
"That means less privacy for us both-And no more or at least less sleepovers here with your friends" I warned him.

He stepped closer to me.
"I don't care! You are MY brother and I'd rather have no sleepovers for the rest of my life if it meant I could still see you! You are not the only one who has always wanted a brother! I've waited ten years and am NOT going to give you up for anything" William shouted. He flopped back down on the rug.

"Things are going really fast" William admitted. I sighed and

sat down cross legged in front him.
"It shows how well we get on, the fact that we can deal with anything that gets thrown at us" I told him. I asked him to hold on whilst I sent Amy a message confirming that William was safe and located. Amy and Barry then let Shaun and everyone else know. Shaun then notified the staff at everywhere we had been looking for William.

"What moment has stood out for you?" William asked me.
"When you hugged me" I said.
"Huh?".
"It was a big moment for both of us. It showed you really trusted me and that you knew I would comfort you and stick by you" I exclaimed. William shrugged.
"I just felt that I needed a hug off you" William admitted.
"You'd just gone through all that at school, it's only natural you'll have wanted supporting, and I'm more than happy to support you in whatever way you need" I told him.
"You don't want another hug, do you?" He teased. I laughed and shook my head.
"Do you?" I asked, just to make sure he was not covering up. He shook his head.

"I want to say something, something brothers feel about each other but find it hard to admit to the other. I love you Freddy, the way you look after me when I'm scared or upset, the way you laugh along with me when I'm in my cheeky mood, the way you help me when I need it" William said. A tear came to my eye.
"I love you too, you have made me a better person, gotten me to admit things I never could. I'm proud and honoured to call you my brother" I replied.

This time I decided to make the first move and put my arms around his shoulders, I could feel they were still rising and falling a little. He put his arm around my shoulders too.

"So, are you ready for me?" William asked, giggling.
"I don't know, how annoying are you going to be?" I teased, winking at him.
"Depends how lucky you are but can't make any promises!" He joked back. I shoved his head a little.
We both laughed.
"It's going to be tough adjusting, but you know what...I'm really looking forward to living here" I admitted to my brother.
"I'm looking forward to living with my brother" William said. I nodded and smiled.

"So, what do you say we go downstairs?" I asked William. He thought and nodded nervously.
"Hey, I'm going to be there the whole time, right next to you. This involves me too. Just be honest and tell them!" I said. He smiled.
"Have you told them about this space?" William asked. I shook my head.
"No, I asked if I could come and talk to you in private and they went downstairs" I assured him.
"Thanks Freddy" He said.
"Any time".

<u>*15*</u>

We left the stone room with William leading, I made sure the wall was put back into place.

We walked downstairs side by side. He hesitated by the living room door; we could hear Amy and Barry talking quietly to one another. I put my hand on his shoulder. He looked down at it and smiled. He went into the room with me following.

Amy and Barry looked as we entered and sat on the soft chairs in front of them.

"I'm sorry for running off" William said. "It was wrong of me to worry you all like that".

"All we want to know is why you ran off?" Amy asked him. William looked at me. I looked back at him and nodded at him.

"I thought Freddy was going with him. I thought he was leaving my life already" William admitted.

"Darling, he's..." Amy started.

"Mum...I know. Freddy's talked to me and explained everything he could" William told her. She and Barry looked surprised at us both.

"Freddy, we would really like it if you would consider coming to live with us. I know it'd be a lot of change..." Barry asked. I interrupted.

"I would like that too; it's going to be fun!" I admitted.

"Yeah, I'm really looking forward to it" William agreed.

"That's great guys!" Barry exclaimed.

"Now, Freddy, we're not going to make you tell us where William was under one condition?" Barry asked.

"Yeah?".

"That he's safe at all times, wherever he is, and that since you are moving here, you will be able to gain access at any time? The last one both of us must agree to" Barry declared to us both.

"He's safe at all times, just gives him some space but nothing unsafe. I checked it out myself" I reassured them both. They nodded.

"What about the last point?" Amy asked.

"William, will you agree to always let me enter to talk to you?" I asked him quietly.

"If I need it, will you give me space first?" William asked me, nervously.

I nodded.

"I'll come and check on you, then if you want, I'll leave you to it. When you want to talk, just ask" I told my brother.

"You know, you can use it too, when you need space or when we both do" William offered me. I thanked him.

"So?" Amy asked again.

"Yes, we will both always have access to the secret space" William said to his parents. I smiled, so did his parents. There was a knock on the door.

Barry went to answer it. Barry came back in followed by Uncle Andy.

"William, this is our Uncle Andy, he's looked after me all these years" I introduced William to him.

"Uncle Andy, this is William" I told him. They nodded and shook hands.

"Right. We are here to arrange a plan moving forward. Are we okay to talk about this together now?" Barry asked us.

We all exchanged glances and nodded.
"Freds, Of course you know I'll be moving abroad. I'm looking to do this in two months. In-between now and then, it would be a good idea for you to get used to not seeing me every day, although we will still talk loads!" Uncle Andy told me.

I nodded.
"I have talked to Uncle Andy and Barry and got their agreement. If William and you are okay with it, we think it would be a good idea if Freddy lived here every other day and at Uncle Andy's the other days for a month. Then for the last month, mostly stopping here" Amy suggested, looking at me.
"Would you both be happy with that?" Uncle Andy asked William and me.

William and I answered at the same time: "Yes!".
The grown-ups exchanged quick glances.
"Are you sure?" Barry asked, "That was very quick".
"Freddy talked to me about it earlier when he found me. We're both looking forward to living together and being a family" William admitted to his Adoptive parents. Amy and Barry smiled and gave William a big hug.

Uncle Andy then looked at Amy.
"Amy, you have something to talk with Freds about?" He said. She nodded and went ahead.
"Freddy, of course, since you are moving in, you might be confused at what you can call us, especially when we're in public" Amy said. I nodded.
"Well, to answer your future worries, we, including Andy, don't mind what you call us. You can just call us by our names-and if in the future, you want to call us anything else, great" Barry told me. I smiled.

"I'll see what I think" I told them. They nodded understandingly.

"Now, this is NOT going to be easy, especially for you, Freddy. You might not realise how much I'm in your life now, but we will both feel it!" Uncle Andy warned me. I nodded slowly.

"We're of course going to start on your passport application within the next week to ensure it's all sorted for when I do move. I will then pay for you to come and see me and your cousins every year, we'll be coming down to this area every year too, staying in a guest house" Uncle Andy explained to me. I smiled and nodded.

"When I come and see you, can I bring William with me?" I asked. William looked at me. I saw by his face; he was hyped by that idea!
Uncle Andy exchanged glances with Amy and Barry.
"I would like that-Most probably!" William said, with a big smile.
"Depends how much you annoy me beforehand; I might forget to buy you a return ticket" I exclaimed. He stuck his tongue out and blew a raspberry at me. The others laughed.

"Now, that would really be down to Amy and Barry. We'd also have to look into the legality of it" Uncle Andy informed me.
"We trust you Freddy" Barry said suddenly. Uncle Andy looked at him, so did William and me.
"We would trust you with the responsibility of taking William abroad-As long as you were both really careful" Barry clarified.
"Thanks, that means a lot to me" I told Barry. He nodded and smiled.
"You've become a big part of mine and Amy's lives, not just

William's and it's been a great ride" Barry told me. I whirled my head around to wipe tears from my eyes. The grown-ups laughed.

Uncle Andy explained that he was going to have to sell the house we have lived in to fund his Czech life. I looked down and nodded.
"I am going to be able to fund two trips with a removal truck" Uncle Andy told me. "Amy's going to take smaller things in her car".
"Any furniture that Freddy really wants to keep that will not fit in the house, we've got a storage locker that it can be put into, so he will not lose them totally" Amy told Uncle Andy and me.
"We'll also be sorting the house out. Some of the furniture might be able to go around the house, as well as their bedroom. Plus..." Barry added.

"What?" William asked.
"Well, we were going to wait but...We've bought an extension for the back of the house, it will extend the back-utility room and give Freddy his own room!" Amy told us. I saw William's face drop.
"Erm Mum...Can we..." William tried asking. I nodded at him; William saw this.
"Can we extend my bedroom and share? I was really looking forward to doing so and Freddy said he was too" William asked.

"I did say that, and I was! I was just giving William the chance to say it himself as I knew he was trying to" I explained. William nodded and smiled.
Amy and Barry exchanged glances.
"I told you!" Barry said to Amy. This time Amy did roll her eyes.

"Of course we can, if that's what you both really want? If you changed your mind later, it could take a while to separate the room permanently" Amy warned us. William and I looked at each other and nodded.
"Thanks Amy, thanks Barry!" I said.

They both smiled.
"We will of course ask you to watch William whilst we're out and you are in" Amy told me.
"No problem, it'll be an honour" I replied.

"When should we start this?" Uncle Andy asked. Amy looked at him.
"I'd have no issues with Freddy stopping here from tonight except the air bed we keep for William's sleepovers is burst. I don't like any sleeping on the sofa you see" Amy revealed.
William then spoke up: "We could just sleep head to toe until we can get another bed. That's what Ben and I used to do before the air bed".
"You both still do it sometimes to this day! How do you think the air bed burst...?" Barry said. William looked at him.
"That is not something I'd recommend due to Freddy's size; it might be a bit uncomfortable!" Amy started.

Barry burst out laughing.
"Oiii, what are you trying to say?" I teased.
"That you'd break the bed" William jumped in on to the joke, sticking out his tongue at me. I gave him a shove.
"You all know full well...what I meant!" Amy said, rolling her eyes. "Back to being serious, that decision is really up to you two. I know William would be okay so I'm not worried" Amy explained. William nodded.

"What about you, Freddy? Would you be okay with that, just for tonight? I'll spend the next couple of days hunting for a

spare bed" Barry asked me.
"It might be a struggle to sleep if you have not slept like that before" Amy warned. I smiled.
"I've slept head to toe a few times with my cousins, not recently but I should be okay. I'm willing to give it ago" I told them. They both nodded and smiled.

"So, from tonight, yeah?" I asked everyone. I looked at Uncle Andy.
"Yes, from tonight" He agreed.
"That would be great!" Amy agreed.
The grownups all nodded.
"So maybe here on Wednesdays, Fridays, Sundays and whereabouts would you like to spend the seventh day?" Amy asked.
I saw William with his fingers crossed.
"Can I be here on a Monday too please?" I asked politely.
"Cool!" Amy said. William smiled.
"And so, mine on Tuesdays, Thursdays and Saturdays?" Uncle Andy asked. I nodded and smiled.
"If that's okay with you?" I asked. He nodded.

"Of course it is. And don't forget, I will always be here for you, just on the other end of the phone instead of face to face" Uncle Andy told me. I smiled and gave my Uncle a hug.
We spoke for another fifteen minutes before deciding to put the plans into action.

Amy drove Uncle Andy, William and me to Uncle Andy's house. We walked in through the door. Amy and Uncle Andy walked through to the kitchen for a drink while William and I went up to my room. I opened the door.
"And...This is my room!" I told him.
"Thanks for telling me, I might not have known" William

said, with a smirk on his face. I gave him a small shove against the wall. He laughed.

William helped me pack some things to take back to Amy's tonight. We packed stuff like clothes, deodorant, laptop, tablet, chargers, spare toothbrush, some books, Body wash, college work, etc. William immediately packed the rest of my cars, buses, and trucks as well as my old town mat. "Oh cool, good to know you've got your priorities worked out then!" I said. He laughed sarcastically. However, he understood how this would be a hard time for me so was actually very caring and helpful-mostly!

16

William finished packing the cars and everything, then my wash things and my tablet.

"Ready?" He asked me, with a light smile. I closed the box I had been packing and nodded. I put my laptop bag on top of the box.

"Yeah" I said, picking up the box. William stood in front of me.

"You sure?" He asked. I smiled and nodded. He smiled and led the way out of my room carrying two bags himself. We put the stuff down on the final stair before I led the way to the kitchen. Uncle Andy and Amy had been talking.

They looked up when they noticed that we had entered.

"You both okay?" Amy asked us. I nodded, so did William.

"And, Freddy, are you happy with everything including the plans we've discussed today?" Uncle Andy asked me. I thought and nodded.

"Of course, it'll be sad that I won't see you much, but I've got my brother and Amy and Barry and Danny to help me through this..." I told him.

"Who's Danny?" William asked me, looking confused.

"My college tutor, your Mum has met him" I explained. It was now 6p.m.!

We decided to get the show on the road.

"You are doing great Freddy" Uncle Andy told me as he walked us to the front door.

"Thanks, but I promise, I will miss you" I told him, a single tear in my eye.

"That's understandable Freds" He replied. Amy picked up the box whilst I carried my laptop and a present off Uncle Andy for us both that we were to open when we got in.

William carried the two bags he had packed for me. We put everything in the boot. I gave Uncle Andy a big hug before I got into the car, once again sitting with William. Uncle Andy waved us off, with us all waving back.

"Freddy, do you like KFC?" She asked curiously.
"Yeah?" I told her.
"Do you want to go there now? You, William, me and Barry?"
"Sure, that'd be great thanks" I told Amy. She smiled.
"Aren't you gonna ask William?" I asked.
"No need" She answered simply.
William turned to me.
"KFC is my favourite!" He told me.
We went back to the house and picked Barry up. I knew Uncle Andy hated KFC anyway, in fact, he hated most fast foods apart from ham and cheese pizzas from Dominoes.

Twenty minutes later, we were eating our meals inside KFC. It was really nice and not too loud either. We all talked, and we were getting along fantastically. My phone buzzed. I checked it, sighing once I had done so. It certainly did surprise me. With great timing, William went to toilet.

I showed his parents the text I had just received:
'Hi. I'm ready to tell him'.
They stared at the text.
"Does that mean...Ben wants to tell William, after all?" Barry asked me. I nodded.
"Yeah, I believe I might have had something to do with it...God, this is going to be very difficult" I admitted. Amy nodded sadly.
"I'm glad he's doing it though" I added. Amy nodded again, along with Barry.

William came back from the toilet. As he sat down, I spoke up.
"Do you wanna go see Ben tonight after we've finished? We can tell him the news" I asked him. I did not want to tell him the tragic news as Ben wanted to. William smiled.
"Yeah!" William replied.

Barry and Amy exchanged glances.
"And we'll leave the room again-so you boys can talk and play again, if you want?" Amy asked William. William nodded and thanked her. Whilst Amy was talking to William, I took my phone out.
'Hi Ben, that's really brave of you. We're coming by after we finish our dinner. I will text you when we're on our way. Do you want any of us there when you tell him?' I sent the text to Ben.
'Maybe you, if that's okay? Our talk the other day really helped and think you'll be able to help us communicate about this. Talking about emotions and feelings isn't my strong point. Phil said to come any time before 9pm' Came Ben's reply. I sent a thumbs up emoji before returning my phone to my pocket.

We got into the car 15 minute later, all stuffed from our food. Despite the amount of food I had just ate, my chest felt as if it contained a blackhole. I texted Ben like I promised and told him we were on our way.

As we entered the hospital, we bumped into Peter.
"Hi Peter, what are you doing here?" William asked.
"A cousin I'm very close with is having a baby. She wanted me and Mum to be the first people to meet him" He explained with a smile.
"Cool! I'm here to see my best friend, Ben" William told him.
"Oh, that boy that had just left when I met you?" Peter

remembered. William smiled and nodded.

"Right, well, we shouldn't keep them waiting. I'll see you in a bit" Peter said, walking quickly down a corridor, waving.

We waved back. We made our way to the children's ward and to Ben's room. I knocked on the door.

"Come in!" Ben shouted. I poked my head in and smiled faintly.

"Are you ready?" I mouthed to Ben. He nodded. I smiled faintly again and opened the door fully. Barry, Amy, William, and I strolled into the room. We exchanged greetings to him and vice versa. About ten minutes later, Barry and Amy went to the hospital restaurant. Ben was feeling okay, so he sat on the edge of the bed. His legs and feet swinging backwards and forwards.

I could sense it.

This was it.

"William...I have to tell you something..." Ben started. He was struggling to look at William.

"What's wrong?" William asked. The three of us were sitting on the side of Ben's bed with William in the middle.

"A lot. I couldn't tell you before. I'm..." Ben tried. I looked at them both. William was getting lots of tears in his eyes.

I knew he had just figured out what Ben was trying to tell him.

"How long?" William asked, tearfully.

"They don't know for sure. They estimate under three weeks" Ben told William, his voice breaking.

"That gives us three weeks" William suggested. I sighed. William looked at me, Ben did too.

"It isn't as simple as that. William, he could..." I started.

"...I might not be here tomorrow or next week. Plus, the

longer I do last, the weaker I'll get. Even if I were to last those full three weeks, I would likely be in deep pain" Ben explained. Williams shoulders sagged like jelly and his eyes weld up. I could tell Ben was trying not to fall apart too.

Ben had had to get back into bed.
I went and sat on the other side of Ben's bed.
"You are allowed to cry" I told him quietly.
"I have to be brave" He cried softly.
"Bravery isn't about crying or being afraid or worries, it's about how much you let the bad things win and if you let them change you. Crying is very brave and shows you care" I reassured them both.

William looked at me.
"You knew, didn't you?" He asked me. I nodded sadly.
"He told me when he had asked to speak to me in private, when I first met him" I admitted to him.
"Why didn't you tell me!" William cried. Standing up and stepping towards me.
"Because I told him not to" Ben told him, tears in his eyes.

"Why would you do that?" William asked.
"Because, you are my best friend. I didn't want our friend relationship to change. I was frightened of showing you emotion and that I was frightened" Ben said looking down at his bed sheets.

William walked up to his bed and got on next to him. He wrapped his arms around his ill friend. Ben did the same. I smiled and was so proud of them. I walked out of the room and ensured the privacy slide was on. Anyone including nurses had to knock before they entered when it was in force. Obviously, it does not apply during emergencies. I went and got a can of Fanta from the vending machine up the corridor. I got Ben one too. William had got a Sprite on the way in.

"You are Freddy Lewis, right?" A voice asked. I spun around. It belonged to a teenager around my age. He observed me.
"Yeah" I said. He stepped a step closer.
"I am Oscar Richy, Ben's brother" He introduced himself.
"I didn't know he has a brother" I admitted.
"I am not surprised. I have not been in his life much. I live and work hundreds of miles away. Yeah, I'm older than I look!" He admitted. I nodded.
"So, William, Ben's best friend, is your brother?" Oscar asked. I nodded again.

"He is a lucky boy" Oscar told me. I sighed.
"What's wrong?".
"I've made so many mistakes. Was I right not to tell William about Ben...?" I said.
"Only you can answer that. Was that a mistake? What are they doing now?" He asked.
"They're consoling one another. Ben's told William just now" I told Oscar.
"I know, our parent's have gone to the canteen to give them so privacy" Oscar explained, "He told me it was you that convinced him".
I nodded and smiled softly.
"Sometimes...The only options are hard or cold ones...But you still have to choose" Oscar told me. I looked down.

17

It was four days later. I had stopped at William's when we had come back from the hospital, stopped at Uncle Andy's the night after, then stopped with William again. Barry had gotten an 'as new' fold up bed from a charity shop, for the second night I stopped there. It was really neat!

I arrived at college early, it had been closed for the past few days due to a 'safety' issue. I went into the empty classroom. I took my seat and waited for a sign of life. Danny came into the room.
"Hi Freddy, you're early?" He said.
"You don't have to be THAT surprised" I exclaimed.
"Sorry bud, how are you?" He asked, coming towards me. He stopped in front of me with his hands in his pockets.

"William's best friend is dying. William only found out the other day" I informed him. He sighed.
"Do you know him too?" Danny asked. I nodded.
"Yeah, William introduced me to him the first day he could have visitors. We got on straight away. He told me that day that his problem was terminal. I couldn't tell William" I told Danny.
"Of course, it would have been hard to..." Danny started. I sighed.
"No, I literally couldn't. Ben had asked me not to tell him!" I explained. He nodded sadly.

"I just don't know how I can help William with this. I told them both that they are allowed the cry and be emotional, but I'm trying to be strong for their sake" I admitted. He sat down in the chair next to me.
"You too can show emotion, I get that you are trying to

hold it together, so William and Ben do but...It's about finding the right balance. They will both be turning to you. By the sounds of it: They look up to you" Danny said.

"They really should have picked a better role model!" I sighed. Danny looked me right in my eyes.
"I don't think that would have been possible" He said quietly. I looked up at him and gave him a small smile. The door opened, and my fellow students started coming in. Danny stood up and greeted them all.

"Now everyone's here, we'll get started. We're going to work on the different parts of a computer like the central processing unit and the random actual memory" Danny announced. "Freddy, you have already done a lot of this unit, so I would like you to work in the shop today, if you are up for that of course?" Danny asked me. I smiled and nodded. He got everyone else set up before giving me the shutter key, lunch voucher and sending me on my way down. I went to the café quickly and got a couple of bottles of apple juice and water for the day. As long as we kept them away from the electrical things, we were fine to drink in the shop, if it had a lid.

I opened the shutter and went inside. I set the shop computer up and turned everything else on. The first customer came to me ten minutes later:
"Hi, my laptop is running really slow and these security alerts keep on popping up although I have protection installed" The guy explained to me. I nodded.
"Okay, I'm Freddy by the way. I'm happy to take a look and see if I can locate and fix the problem. Do you have all your personal files backed up?" I asked. He nodded.

"Great. Nothing should happen to them and we are not allowed to view any personal files without your permission in accordance with the data protection act. Although in case of accidents since we are trainees, we always recommend that you make copies of everything as we cannot be held responsible for the loss of personal files, unless we have been overly negligent" I told him clearly.

"No worries, I completely understand" He told me. I smiled and reached behind me for a slip.

"Right, could you fill this out for me please and I'll get the item booked in?" I said. He filled it in and we both signed it. I tore the front two slips off. I keep the top one and he keeps the bottom one.

"So how does this work then? Do I come back tomorrow or something?" The customer, named Mr Tyne asked.

"What we do is: Once I have booked each item in, I take a look at it myself. If I need help or can't do whatever is needed, I will speak to my tutor about the problems. Simply, we give you a call on the phone number that you provide on this slip when it's ready to be collected. We might also ring you if we need any more information" I explained. He smiled and thanked me again before walking out of the college.

I took the laptop in and booked it in using the shop computer. I loaded up the customers laptop. I noticed it took a bit of time to load. I logged on using the password I had been given. I installed different programmes and investigated some suspicious programmes on the computer. I made a list of those I would recommend taking off or looking in to. I loaded up his anti-virus software. It looked fairly good but some of the settings were a right mess and were not scheduled to do any automatic scans. The last scan was four months ago! I started a full computer scan.

I heard loads of footsteps advancing. It was a group of high school kids. They appeared to be on a school trip. It took a moment to recognise the one who was now waving to me. Peter. I waved back.

The college staff member leading the tour lead them to the shop desk. Now I remembered that there was a part of the college for teenagers between the ages of 14 and 16.
"This is the college's computer repair shop. It is open to the public as well as the students and staff of the college. We have a number of friendly students who work in here lead by their tutor Danny. Would you like to explain a bit about what you do in here, what you think about your course and the college's facilities?" She asked me.

"My name's Freddy Lewis, I've been at the college since September. I love being here, all the tutors I've met have been nice and knowledgeable. The shop itself opened a couple of months ago and it's been really cool helping people. It might be best if anyone wants to ask me any specific questions?" I recommended.

The staff member nodded and motioned for the high school students to feel free to ask me anything.
"How does being down here and working in the shop affect your college work?" A boy about Peter's age asked me.
"It doesn't. In a way, this shop is part of my college course work! It allows me to complete many of the units of my course faster and more fun than working out of textbooks" I explained. He nodded and thanked me.

"How does college compare to school?" An older girl asked.
"You mean like as in drinking, taking breaks, listening to music whilst you're working?" I asked. She nodded. I smiled.
"Of course, you are still here to learn and do classes. On average though, they are more lenient than schools are. As long as you are careful, you can drink water or juice in the

classrooms here, not allowed to eat. If you ask the tutor if you can go outside for some fresh air for a moment, they'll most probably say yes. I often listen to music when I don't need to use my ears", I told her. She smiled and thanked me.

I saw Peter put his hand up. The college staff nodded at him. "Yeah, I've heard that there are facilities available on an evening or weekend if you need extra help revising?" Peter asked me.
"I have attended a couple of the Saturday ones. It's mostly a space to revise and complete coursework without distractions. There's a schedule available that says which tutors will be present each day. The rules are more relaxed but obviously safety rules still apply. I'd certainly look into it if you do come to the college!" I recommended. He nodded.

"Right, we are going to take a break now, feel free to use the toilets, they are down the corridor there and of course the café is right here" The college staff member said.

While all the other high school students sat down or went to the café, Peter came up to me.

18

"I didn't know you went here? How are you?" He asked with a smile.
"Yeah, I'm not too bad thanks. Just my personal life is getting tough" I admitted.
"How come?".
"Some people I know aren't going to be around for much longer" I told him. He nodded.
"You're coping very well with it" Peter said. I thanked him.

A teacher from the high school came up to us.
"Sorry guys, I just have to ask for obvious reasons: Do you know each other?" He asked us.
"Yeah, my neighbour is his brother. They actually met because of this shop!" Peter explained.
"How?" The teacher asked curiously.
"Well, it's not part of the college curriculum, I can tell you that much!" I joked. They laughed.

"His Mum was the shop's first customer. My tutor had asked me if I'd clean the shop before the official opening the next week. He still owes me a favour for that! Anyway, as I was cleaning, this woman came to the counter. I wasn't meant to be fixing computers that day, but she seemed desperate for hers to work as soon as possible so I did it as a good deed" I explained. they nodded.

"She came back later. The laptop's screensaver was of a boy. The woman and I had just got talking and she mentioned her son, so I asked her if the boy was him. It was. My uncle has been my guardian since I was three. After talking a bit more, we confirmed he is my brother" I revealed.

"Okay then guys, I'll leave you to it. You haven't got long though before we'll be moving on" The teacher said. He walked away, towards the toilets.

Peter turned back to me.

"What's this news you were talking about?" Peter asked.

"I don't know if it's my place to tell people. It's about William's friend, Ben" I told him. He looked at me.

"I went to see him after my cousin was born. He was asleep, but his Mum told me that he's terminal. She and his Dad had been in the canteen to give the boys their privacy whilst they talked about it all" Peter informed me.

"I'm sure she told you that he only told William the other day, he was really nervous about doing so but I am so proud of them both. They did really well handling it" I explained. Peter nodded.

"No, she didn't mention that. She mentioned you guys had dropped by again. Of course, I explained that I had seen you at the entrance".

"I've also started living with William and his adoptive family most days. My uncle is moving to Czech Republic to look after his other kids" I told Peter.

"Wow! I love the Czech Republic! It's so cool. I have a distant cousin who lives there" Peter told me, with enthusiasm.

"Is it wrong that I kind of hate the place?" I asked him.

"Of course not. I know what you're thinking" Peter claimed. I looked at him.

"You are thinking that the Czech Republic is stealing your uncle, who's basically been your Dad for the past fifteen years" He said. I looked down and nodded. Peter put a hand on my shoulder.

"You are allowed to be upset about it, and you are allowed to show it. There are people all around you that care about you. Please don't fight this alone" He told me. He then took his hand off my shoulder and walked back to his group as they headed towards the stairs.

I stood there deep in thought for a moment. I blinked. I then went back to the customers laptop. The scan had finished so I went onto the clean ups and optimizations. A woman came up to the counter.
"Hi, can you help me install programmes on to my laptop?" She asked.
"Sure, I can! As long as they are lawful" I said. She laughed.
"Don't worry, I'm talking about anti-virus software and an alternate office programme" She explained.

I nodded and smiled.
"Yeah, that should be fine. My name's Freddy by the way. I can do it with you now and offer you further advice if you want or I could take it in and do it?" I offered. "I would recommend the first one".
"Can you show me, so I know how to do it next time please?".
"Sure. Can you please fill in this slip and sign it at the bottom please?" I asked, handing her a slip.
"Do I need to leave a number?"
"Err no, just put you're not leaving it here with us" I advised.

She nodded and finished filling it in. I took the slip in and gave her a copy of it. I also logged the job on the shop computer.
I spent about 20 minutes installing software on to her computer, showing her how to do so and answering questions she had. She waved goodbye to me with me waving back. I turned my attention back to the other customers laptop.

It had finished doing everything I had wanted. I shut the laptop down and turned it back on. I observed it loaded up quicker than it had done the first time. I started one more anti-virus scan to double check everything was okay. Whilst it did so, I shut the shutters and got my lunch from the café.

I opened the shutters just high enough for me to get back in the shop, leaving them halfway closed. I ran up the customer of the laptop and told him it was ready for collection in about an hour. I put the laptop out of view and locked it away before closing the shutter fully and going to see Danny. I showed him the list of suspicious programmes and he agreed with my recommendations. The customer came and collected the laptop about half an hour before I left college.

I got back to Uncle Andy's, the clock on the passageway table reading: 3:25p.m. Uncle Andy was sitting on the sofa watching a series he likes. He smiled when I came in.
"How was college today?" He asked.
"Brilliant thanks, I worked in the shop again and saw Peter, William's neighbour" I said, sitting at the other end of the sofa. He nodded.
"Do you want any help packing when you start?" I asked him.
"You can if you want?" He told me.
"I think it might help me accept and ease into the fact that you are leaving. I haven't been in denial as such, but deep down, I wasn't really thinking about it" I admitted. He put an arm around my shoulder.
"Remember what I said, it's going to be hard! You are allowed to go through these stages. I do agree through, that helping me to pack might help us" Uncle Andy agreed. I nodded and smiled.

"How are you feeling this system is going so far?" Uncle Andy asked. I thought about it.

"I've loved staying with William, Amy and Barry. They are really cool, and I'm getting to know them more everyday I'm there" I replied. Uncle Andy smiled and gave me a high five.

"Well done Freds, I'm so proud of you" He exclaimed.

We just spent the evening watching films and ate some snacks we had had in for a bit.

<u>*19*</u>

I walked to the hospital with William. It was few days later and he had wanted to visit Ben alone without his parents. They agreed.
"Of course, as long as you stick to Freddy" Barry had said.
"We completely understand. Freddy, if you can keep on texting us and let us know when you get to the hospital and when you leave?" Amy had asked me. I had nodded and then we were off. We had ridden the bus most of the way; then we decided to walk the rest of the way. We started talking quietly about ten minutes away from the hospital.

"Have you enjoyed being with me, I mean living with us?" He asked suddenly. I stopped and looked at him.

"Yes, I've loved every minute. Before I met you, I didn't know what I had missed. Now I know you, I'm even more annoyed that I didn't get to meet you sooner" I told him. He smiled.
"Why did you ask?" I asked.

He looked at me, then down at his feet quickly.
"Wanted to make sure. I think I'm still nervous-About giving you a good impression of me" He admitted. I turned to him.
"I've been feeling the same" I admitted back.
"We need to accept that we really get along and like each other as we are. We know we're not perfect. We enjoy spending time together. Whether that's talking, playing, supporting each other or even teasing one another as brothers do" William said to me. I smiled and put my hand high into the air. He jumped and slapped me a high five. We were in front of the hospital.

"Come in" Ben called. I could tell by his voice that he was weaker. I saw by William's face that he had noticed too. I took a deep breath and stepped into the room with my brother in tow.

"Hi William, hi Freddy!" He greeted us. I could tell it had cheered him up to see William!

"Hi" William said. Ben motioned for William to come to him. He did, and Ben wrapped his arms around William.

Obviously, William was still upset seeing his best friend like this, but it seemed to have helped him a lot.

"How are you doing?" I asked.

"Oh, I'm thinking of doing a marathon!" Ben joked. We both laughed.

"I meant...How are you taking everything?" I explained. He looked down and back up at me.

"Some of the time, I feel great and understand everything, other times...Other times, I'm so scared. I don't know what to say or do. I don't know when I'm going to... or when the last time I'm going to see someone is. I...I don't even know if it's going to hurt!" Ben told me, his voice getting high. I nodded understandingly. I knelt on the floor near his head.

"Ben, you are... you know. You are allowed to be petrified, nervous and everything in between. We are here for you and will be until the very very end and even afterwards. Meeting you has changed me, it reminded me what bravery looks like and how it improves the attitudes of all those around you. It's also been pretty cool meeting someone who could be even smarter than me" I told him, the last bit with a laugh. He let a tear drop down his cheek. I gave him a big hug. He wrapped his arms around me very tightly. I had to get on the bed in order to reach him, so I had taken my shoes off. I obviously did not want to get mud on his sheets. He let go of me and asked me if we could stay with him for a bit and watch a film. I went outside of the room and talked with a nurse. I went back into the room.

"We are here for as long as you want us here. Due to your circumstances, visiting hours, as such, don't apply to you now, if we don't get in the way of the hospital's work. All we must do is keep on letting Amy know that we are okay. I've got a house key and money for a taxi back" I told Ben, sitting on the bed. William put on 'Ice Age 5' and sat on the other side. I could tell that Ben was feeling supported and comforted. There was a knock at the door half an hour later. I was now sitting in a chair; William was still on the bed.

Ben paused the film and sat up.
"Come in?" He called. The door opened. I saw the confused look on Ben's face.
"Oh, hi Danny" I greeted him, getting up and going over to him. William knew who he was now.
"Ben, this is my college tutor. Whilst I didn't go into detail, I explained how a friend wasn't very well" I explained Ben.
"So, does he know I'm terminal?" Ben asked me. I nodded.

"Do you want me to go? I won't mind" Danny asked Ben. He shook his head and smiled.
"Let's just say that Ben isn't the shy type!" William remarked.
"Just like you then!" I said to William. He stuck his tongue out. Ben laughed.
"Freddy's told me how brave you are being and just wanted to drop this card and offer the best wishes off everyone at Portsmouth college where Freddy goes" Danny explained, handing him a card and a little present. I saw Ben's face light up.

"I'm just going to get a drink" William said.

"I better come too since you don't seem to know how to use those machines!" I exclaimed. We both walked out of the room.

"God, why didn't we get him anything. I'm SUPPOSED to be his best friend!" William cried, when we were near the drink machine.

"I feel exactly the same, usually I would have thought about that but with all the questions I've been asking myself..." I told myself out loud.

"We should get him something now" William suggested.

Danny sat in the chair near Ben's bed.

"I'm afraid I've just done something bad" Danny groaned.

"What?" Ben asked. Danny hesitated.

"Well...I think the boys might be a bit upset that they didn't bring you anything".

Ben rolled his eyes.

"Come on, that's how people feel. I'm going to tell you something, something I shouldn't: The main reason why Freddy told me about you is that he wanted to know the best way he could support you and William. He's finding it really hard too as although you're not any relation, you have become quite a big part of his life and he's become a big part of yours" Danny told Ben.

Ben just sat thinking.

"Surely they know that..." Ben started.

"Tell them" Danny said, before leaving the room and exiting the hospital.

I got back to the room first because William had to go to toilet. I knocked on the door.

"Come in" Ben said. I went in. Ben looked at me.

"How are you?" I asked.

"Still planning on that marathon" Ben said. I stuck my

tongue out at him.

"Freddy, Danny told me..." Ben started.
"Oh, Cra..." I started, dropping into the chair. He cut me off just in time.
"He explained that you weren't sure on how to support me" Ben told me. I nodded and shrugged.
"I didn't know what having needles placed into various parts of my body would be like, I learned. Today, you came in and talked to me with dignity, like an equal and just spent time with me, you have learned too. No matter how smart we are, there'll always be more to learn...Never forget that" Ben told me. I felt myself tearing up. He reached over and gave me another hug.
"And you're not my friend. Like William, you're my brother from another Mother" Ben corrected me. I laughed but stopped soon after.
"I'd be so proud if you were" I admitted to him. He smiled.

"Erm, can you please get me a Fanta please?" Ben asked.
"Is this to get me out whist you talk to William in private?"
"Well, yeah. Now you anticipate my moves" Ben cracked. I laughed and walked out of the room.
"I wasn't joking about the Fanta though; all they give me here is health sh..." Ben shouted. I said okay and closed the door just before the final word could come out completely.

I hid around the corner when I saw William coming. He knocked and went into Ben's room.
"I got you this, I'm so sorry I forgot to bring you something!" William said in a high pitch voice.
Ben looked down at the gift bag and shoved it back at William. William's face looked hurt.
"I liked the first gift that I was given!" Ben said. William had formed tears.

"The one when I first moved here, three years ago. I met a young boy called William Jamme and he took the new kid in to his life and made sure he found out his area. He had sleepovers with a kid he barely knew, to help him feel included. How dare you think that you haven't got me anything! Meeting you was my biggest gift of all and always will be" Ben told my brother, His voice raising in parts. William looked at his friend, them both had tears in their eyes. William rushed up to him. They wrapped their arms around each other's shoulders tightly.

"William, this is going to kill you and me both but...I don't want to see you again. My condition is going to get worse and do not want you to see me like that. I might not even be able to remember my best friend one day" Ben told William honestly. William laughed.
"Oh, you were being serious. I am not going to abandon you just because things are getting hard! You mean too much to me and you are and will always be my best friend forever! I WILL be here until the very end and beyond" William made it truly clear to him. Ben nodded and gave a light smile.

There was a knock on the door.
"Come in" Ben said. I entered the room.
"Is everything okay?" I asked them both. The boys exchanged glance and nodded. Still, I could see tear stains on their cheeks. I just nodded and gave Ben his Fanta.
"Thanks Freddy"
"Call me Fred" I told him. I turned to William. "You too".
They both looked happily at me, particularly William. I could tell it made him feel really accepted.

"Can't we call you Scooby instead?" Ben teased. I stuck my

tongue out at him.

"Thanks for everything you both have done today. It has really helped me in lots of ways" Ben admitted to us. We smiled and nodded.

"I think you should get back off home now, so Amy doesn't worry about you both. But, can you come back tomorrow and spend a bit of time with me again please?" Ben asked, mainly looking at William.

"So, do you want me or Amy to drop him off and pick him back up?" I asked him.

He shook his head.

"I meant both of you, although I'd like to lark about with William one to one for a bit too...If that's okay?" He explained. I smiled.

"So, we'll both come again tomorrow and at some point, I'll just pop to the hospital restaurant" I told Ben. He thanked me.

"You're very welcome. Good night Ben, see you tomorrow!" I said.

"See you soon Ben, have a good night. If you want to talk to me, no matter what time it is, you have got our number" William reminded him. Ben nodded and smiled before seeing us to the door. A nurse was at the door and said she would see him back to his bed. We walked away waving with Ben waving back.

20

We got home about twenty minutes later and let ourselves in. We went straight to our room and went straight to bed. I got changed in the bathroom.

"I'm glad I'm sharing a room" William admitted.

"I'm right here to support you, no matter what time it is. If you need to talk, wake me up" I told him. He smiled and said goodnight. I said goodnight before falling straight to sleep.

I was woken up by my phone buzzing. I picked it up. William had somehow remained asleep. I answered the call and got up slowly. I walked into the hallway.

"Hello?" I said. My face dropped and my heart burst into flames.

"Okay thanks. Yes, of course we will" I insisted before cutting off. I took a deep breath. I walked to Amy and Barry's bedroom. I knocked and opened the door.

Barry lifted his head up first.

"Is everything okay Freddy?" He asked.

"Erm no... We need to get to the hospital now. Ben hasn't got long left. He's asked for William" I revealed. This made Amy's head shoot up. We clarified what I had said and they both shot up and got dressed.

I went and woke my brother up whilst I got dressed.

"William..." I tried but could not. His eyes filled up.

"He's..." William figured.

"No but he hasn't got long left. His mind is still with it and he knew this is what you would have wanted to be called and he wanted to see you too...beforehand" I explained. He nodded and shot straight downstairs.

"Aren't you gonna get dressed?" I called. I could tell that was a stupid question and chased after him. We quickly put our shoes on. Amy and Barry where trying to start the car up. It would not go. William was getting increasingly hysterical.

"I'll phone up for a taxi" I offered quickly. They nodded.
I did so, and luckily one was nearby. The taxi pulled up in front of the car. I recognised it immediately.

"Hi guys, this must be William?" Shaun gathered. I nodded.
"Where are you off to at this time?".
"To see a friend at the hospital, he's asked to see us urgently" I explained.
"I'm so sorry to hear that!" He exclaimed. He pulled us up in front of the hospital about five minutes later. I was about to give him the fare, but he shoved it away.
"Quickly...Just go!" He told us. We thanked him and ran down the corridors.

William was far in front, I had to guide him as he was getting too hysterical. I held him in place and told him to take a few deep breaths. He did so and carried on walking, us both breathing softly but deeply. The receptionist saw us and rushed us through to the room.

The room was full of Nurses. They turned to see us enter.
"I'm sorry, he's got about ten minutes. His parents have nipped to the canteen for a few minutes to allow William to say goodbye, but they of course want to be with him when he does go" One of them said. I heard William sob; my heart felt as if it was in a juicer!

"Right. We are now going to leave to allow visitors to say their goodbyes" A nurse announced. They all said goodbye to Ben before walking out. Amy and Barry said goodbye to

Ben and gave him a small hug before leaving the room crying.

This left just me, William, and Ben.
"Deja Vu guys" Ben joked breathlessly. We laughed sadly.
"How?" William asked sobbing.
"I'm sorry but he hasn't got time William. We have to say our goodbyes" I said, tears in my eyes too.
"Something I'm happy about is that you're minds still there, I know that was your worst fear of all" I told Ben.
Ben smiled softly and nodded.

"Ben, you are my inspiration, the voice and strong mind that will keep on telling me to take a risk and be bold, to keep learning. I will never forget you and you will be in my thoughts every day!" I told Ben. He got tears in his eyes.
"Are you in pain?" William asked, I could tell he had to. Ben shook his head, pointing to the tubes in his body.
I gave Ben a hug, he wrapped his arms around me too. I could feel his body shaking.
I grabbed his hand. There was a knock on the door. William went to see. The door opened revealing Peter. He came in. I was about to explain to him what was happening.
"I know" Peter said in a sad tone, "I never got the chance to meet him".
"I'm not done yet!" He said, quite loudly. Peter came closer to Ben.

"Peter, this is my best friend Ben. Ben, this is our neighbour Peter" William introduced them to each other.
"Hi, great to finally meet you" Ben said breathlessly.
"Likewise. I just wanted to meet you, sad it also has to be goodbye less than ten seconds later" Peter told Ben, even him getting a tear in his eye.
"Oh, it's never goodbye. William has lots of stories to share"

Ben declared. William laughed.

"You're so brave, goodbye Ben!" Peter said, not knowing what else to say. He left the room without turning back.

"William, you will always be my best friend" Ben told him. William came forward and grabbed his other hand. I held his other. We both got on the bed at either side and consoled him.

"Ben...Ben, you are always going to be my star, guiding my every move, my every thought. I don't want this to be a spectacular speech. I just want to tell you that I will never forget you and that you are my best friend forever and..." William just wrapped his arms tightly round Ben. Ben was smiling and was happy.

Ben's parents came in.

"William, I'm sorry but we have to go and let his parents have time with Ben" I tell William softly. William would not let go of his friend.

"It's okay if William needs to stay" Ben's Mum said, tearfully. I looked at William and nodded. I said goodbye to Ben before climbing off the bed.

"I can't say anything that'll help...But...I'm so so sorry" I told them, shaking their hands.

"You just did" Ben's Dad said. I took one last look at Ben, he smiled at me and weakly waved goodbye. I do so too before I quickly left the room.

About three minutes later, a nurse came out the room and nodded slightly. She asked if a couple of people could come in and help them console William. Amy said that she and I would try.

Ben's parents were consoling each other at the other end of the room, a nurse was with them. There was also a nurse with William, trying to console him. William would not let go of Ben, he laid on the bed, clutching his best friend. I went out of the room for a minute and returned with a can of Fanta. I placed it next to Ben.

"I'm so sorry William, Ben was a great person" I said to William, standing next to him. He did not look at me, he just clutched Ben very tightly. Some more Nurses came in with a trolley with a giant black bag on top. I knew what this bag was.
"Can we have a few more moments please?" Amy asked them. They nodded understandingly.

The nurses then stepped back towards the door but did not leave the room.
I was holding myself together by thinking to myself that: Ben was no longer in pain and could run around again like he had done before! Plus, I was happy that he got multiple of his final wishes.

Amy slowly went over to William.
"Come on, let's go and get a drink or something?" Amy suggested quietly. A nurse said she could arrange an office for us to sit in and take it in. Barry and I thanked her. Amy's attention was all on William. I went over to him too. William shook his head.
"William..." I started but found that I did not know what to say myself.

Barry came over to me and put an arm around my shoulders. He walked me outside for some fresh air. Amy stayed in the room with William. Danny was coming up towards the entrance. He ran towards me when he saw my condition.
"Oh no" He gasped as he neared us, seeing My and Barry's

faces. He gave me a hug.
Barry and I could tell that he had guessed what had just happened.
"Yeah, he's gone" I confirmed quietly.

He let go of me.
"You both gave Ben some much-needed support and fun, especially last night. He looked like he was truly having a great time" Danny told me. I nodded.
"Where is William?" Danny asked. Barry sighed.
"Still in the room with Ben. He won't leave him" Barry admitted. Danny nodded sadly.
"Maybe Freddy could try talking to him?" Danny suggested.
"I tried, obviously. I just didn't know what to say" I told my tutor. "Then Barry brought me out here".

Peter came up behind us.
"Wanna walk with me for a bit?" He asked me. I smiled sadly and motioned for him to lead the way. I waved to the two men and followed him.
"I heard a bit of what you were saying" Peter told me.
"Well?" I asked.
"I can't tell you what to say, no one can. Only you can know what to do with William" Peter said. I looked at him.
"He's my brother and I don't even know what to say to him!" I exclaimed. Peter held me in place.
"You've just lost someone too. Who says you have to say anything? Your brother needs you now more than ever...Just be his brother" Peter reminded me.

We had walked in a circle and were nearing the entrance again. We walked back to the hospital room. Amy was outside with her head in her hands. The Nurses were outside too, all but one who remained in the room.
I walked up to Amy.

She looked up at me.

"If he doesn't come out in a few minutes, the nurses have said they'll have to physically get him out" Amy said sadly.

"Can I go in please?" I asked her and the Nurses. They all nodded. Peter came in with me.

He stayed near the door, next to the Nurse who had remained in the room.

I walked up to my brother. I took a bold leap of faith and just wrapped my arms around him-and he let go of Ben and wrapped his arms around me too. I motioned for the Nurse to remain where she was.

"Wanna go and have something to drink?" I whispered to William, still holding my Brother. It was killing me not to hold Ben's hand again, but I knew that could make William worse.

William nodded.

"But in the canteen" He whispered back.

I turned his head to look at me.

"Are you sure?" I asked him, quietly. He nodded. I smiled and nodded.

William let go of me and took one more look at Ben. He gave Ben one last hug for a few seconds before coming away. He led the way out with me following very closely behind him. Peter came out too. Before we turned the corner, William turned his head and spoke to the Nurses:

"You can do what you need to do" He said, still tearfully but he was calmer.

"We will look after him William" One of them said back.

William smiled before walking with me to the canteen.

21

It was two days later; School and college had given me and William the week off given the full circumstances. We of course had thought a lot about Ben, but we made sure we mostly had fun and messed about. That is what he would have wanted.

"Can I help you at the shop?" William suddenly asked.
"Huh?" I asked.
"The computer shop at college?" William said. I stood there thinking.
"Are you sure you want to?" I asked.
William thought.
"I do. If it weren't for that place, we wouldn't have met. Plus, it'll give us something to do and get us working together!" William suggested.

That actually sounded good to me. I talked to Barry about William's idea, he confirmed it would be okay with him and Amy. He also explained he would talk to Miss Rodgers about it.

My mobile rang an hour later. I picked it up.
"Hi Freddy" Danny said.
"Oh, hi Danny!".
"How are you and William?" He asked with concern.
"We're getting there. Look, William's asked if he can join me in the college and the shop for a week. I agree it might be good for us both to do something, but we'd still be together for support" I explained to Danny.

"Right. For a start, we'd need written consent off Amy or Barry as well as his school. Next, he would be restricted as

to what tools he could use. And...Anything that he breaks, damages, or does wrong, it could become the responsibility of his parents since he's not a member of the college. If all this can be sorted, I love the idea!" Danny informed us.
We cut off so that I could start all the enquires.

Miss Rodgers called by the house an hour and a half after me speaking to Danny.
"Hi Boys, how are you both doing?" She asked. We exchanged glances and nodded.
"I already miss him so much" William admitted. Miss Rodgers smiled sadly.
"Erm, Would..." I started. The teacher stopped me.
"Barry told me about William's idea, and I've spoken to the school. They are prepared to let William attend the college for a week in exchange for the college letting you come to the school the week after the Easter Holidays. I've asked the College and they've said it's fine with them" Miss Rodgers told us both.

"What do you want me to attend William's school for?" I asked.
"We need help tying down William, so he keeps still in class!" She joked. William's eyes shot invisible lasers out at his teacher. She laughed. I laughed too.
"Nah, A teaching assistant is going to be on pregnancy leave and the kid needs a kind, sensible and really understanding person to help him until she gets back" Miss Rodgers told me.
"Hey, wait a minute! This sounds like you'd be avoiding hiring someone?" Barry asked, suspiciously.

"Yes, we technically would be avoiding that, BUT we are going to provide travel expenses, Freddy's lunch and breakfast, if he wants to come along to the breakfast club.

We will also, of course, pay for his DBS check" Miss Rodgers explained.

"It's a deal. How can I say no to supporting someone. Who is this kid, by the way?"

"Kaleb..."

"Isn't that the kid I helped when he and William was getting picked on?" I remembered. Miss Rodgers nodded. I smiled and shook her hand. She handed us a signed document to give to college.

"Thanks so much!" William said.

"No problem, see you soon!" Miss Rodgers replied before leaving.

We neared the college. I saw William look at me out of the corner of my eye. It was the week after.

"You okay?" I asked. He looked at me and nodded.

"Just a little nervous" William admitted.

"All this is, is a bit of fun and for you to see what I do here. There's no pressure. If you want to end this experience at any point, just tell me or Danny and I will bring you home!" I reassured him. My brother smiled at me. We went into the college. Danny had asked me and William to get in half an hour early so William could talk to him and vice versa.

"Hi Danny" I said, opening the door to our regular classroom. He was sat down at one of the tables.

"Hey guys, come and sit down!" Danny asked. We did.

"Are you sure you both want to do this?" He asked patiently. We nodded.

"Yeah I'm sure" William said.

"Okay. Do you have any questions about the college or what Freddy does here?" Danny asked William.

"How many Fanta breaks does he take?".

"Erm..." I protested.

"About 20...Next" Danny joked. I rolled my eyes.

"Why does Freddy come here for three days a week whilst I have to go to school Five days a week?" William asked. Danny smiled.

"At school you learn a vast variety of subjects. At college, you only learn your chosen option. You can also take an English or maths class in addition if you didn't pass them at school" Danny explained.

We spent about ten minutes answering questions until we began to talk about today's plans.

"Right, this morning, you both will be in the shop. This will give you the chance to watch Freddy running it and how it works. I would strongly recommend not touching customer's computers until you have a bit more knowledge of it all. This afternoon, both you and Freddy, will be up here where we will be refreshing, or in your case, learning our knowledge of computers, repairing them, and speeding them up" Danny explained to William. We both nodded. He gave me the shutter key and two lunch vouchers.

"Here is a notice that permits William to be here and be in the shop. I'm trusting you to read the shops rules as well as the basics of the Data Protection Act and the Computer Misuse Act to William before you open the shop to customers" Danny told me. I smiled and nodded.

"Great. Just, have fun and pay attention to Freddy" The tutor told William. He smiled and thanked him before we both walked down the stairs and across the college towards the booth.

I got William a drink from the café opposite the shop.

"I don't want one at the moment but if I did, would you be okay getting me a drink?" I asked my brother. He nodded. I went up to the shutters to open them.

"Don't you need to stand on anything?" William cracked. I stuck my tongue out at him.
"You're getting a bit cheeky!" I observed.
"It's a matter of joking about before I cry" William told me. I nodded understandingly.
"That observation wasn't an insult or tease by the way" I said. He laughed.

I spent half an hour going through the Data Protection and Computer Misuse acts with William. He completed a couple of worksheets about them. He also took notes about the other stuff. I was really proud and pleased at how mature and serious he was taking this opportunity. I finally opened the screen window above the counter to open the shop.
"How busy does it get?" William asked.
"In here?".
"Yeah" William said, taking a sip of his apple juice.
"Well of course it varies from day to day but it's always steady and not rushed. It's ran be students so we're still learning things" I explained. He nodded.

The first customer came up about fifteen minutes after opening. An elderly man.
"Hi, I was wondering if you could advise me on any courses in Portsmouth that assist older people in learning how to be digital?" He asked.
"Erm yeah. My names Freddy. I know the library on Milton Road and the Portsmouth Central one often does computer courses for over 50's. I've of course never been to one, but I've heard they're good and interesting. To be fair, most libraries should offer these kinds of courses" I revealed.

"I remember seeing a sign in the window of the one on Milton Road, there is one tomorrow afternoon at 1:30p.m." William added. I looked at him and smiled.

"Thanks very much guys, you've been very useful!" He told us both, "Isn't he a bit young for college or is he one of these special gifted lads?".

"Oh no, this is my brother William. He's joining me at the college for the week. It's part of an agreement, after a hard event a few days ago" I explained.
"Well. You are doing really well so far mate" He congratulated him. He wrote some comments on a piece of paper and asked me to pass it on to my tutor and asked neither of us to look ourselves. I gathered it was about William's helpfulness or something.

22

"Hi guys, I'm hoping you can fix school computers?" Another costumer asked. It was about an hour after the elderly gentleman had been. This customer was a woman with a kid at her side. I recognised the kid immediately: Kaleb. I could also tell this woman with him was more than likely his pregnant teaching assistant!

"Hi, I'm Freddy. I'm not entirely sure on that one. I will have to check one that due to policies. Have you got any paperwork or notes from the school about what they want doing to it and when by?" I asked. The assistant rummaged around in her bag and brought out sheets of paper. She handed then to me. I looked it over.

"I also thought it might be a good opportunity for Kaleb to meet you. I know you've kind of met already but I know he wanted to meet you properly and in better circumstances!" Mrs Just, the teaching assistant, explained. Her name was on her badge. I nodded and smiled.

"I tell you what, do you want me to run this up to Danny and see what he says" William asked.
"Hi William" Kaleb said. William waved back.
"That would be fab thanks" I showed my appreciation. William ducked under the counter and walked towards the I.T. department. I still felt nervous about letting him go on his own, but I quickly decided that I could not smother, or bubble wrap my brother. He was ten after all!

"Hi Kaleb, do you remember me?" I asked him softly. He smiled and nodded. He had a great smile.
"Do you understand what's happening soon?" I asked him.

He nodded and whispered into Mrs Just's ear. She turned to me.

"In a nutshell, yes. He knows and understands the basics" She told me.

"So, you are happy for me to cover Mrs Just next week?" I asked patiently. He nodded.

"I... I trust you" He said quietly, so quietly I had difficulty hearing it. I smiled and thanked him.

I turned to Mrs Just.

"Is that all the time off you're having, a week?!" I asked her. She nodded.

"Well, it is the Easter Holidays next week, plus my husband and I want to share the responsibility so are splitting it. He'll be looking after the new one afterwards as the company he works for is closing down" She explained.

"I'm sorry to hear that!" I said. She smiled.

"It's not such a problem as it'll work out for the best. I enjoy my job much better than he does anyway!" She told me.

"Would it be okay to come by yours at some point, so I can get more used to being around you?" Kaleb quietly asked me. I was so shocked that I just looked at Mrs Just.

"I know Miss Rodgers knows and likes you, and to be honest, I have only just met you and already know he'll be unlikely to be in danger around you. Plus, since you are not an official member of staff or even a volunteer at the school yet, I believe it wouldn't be up to us. You would just be helping him as your brother's friend until the DBS check comes back. You would probably just need his Dad's permission as well as whoever owns the house he'd be coming to. I will make some calls now and let you both know what they say" Mrs Just explained. Kaleb nodded.

The teaching assistant turned her eyes on to me.
"How do you like the idea?" She asked me.
"I like it, I think it'll help me to learn how to help you in the classes" I admitted.
"Yeah, that's also an advantage. I did the same, that's likely where he got the idea" Mrs Just said.

"Who else would be there?" He asked me in his quiet voice. I smiled understandably.
"William's parents want to spend some time with William alone tonight and I'm stopping at my Uncle Andy's.
However, he's going to be out from around 4 until 10p.m." I told him. He smiled faintly.
"Would it be okay for me to come during that time then, if school and everyone say yes?" He asked.
I nodded and smiled. "That's why I brought it up. I knew you'd be more nervous around someone you haven't met at all" I explained to him.
"Thanks Freddy, you're a great person" He said. I smiled.
"You are too" I told him.

He looked down.
"Yeah right, I'm scared to death of everything, so quiet people can't hear me, and my quirks are embarrassing!" He argued, in a high tone.
"For starters, everyone is scared of something. Second, I can hear you and I'm partially deaf and lastly, it makes you different and more fascinating, not less. You're better than you think. You just have to unlock it" I assured him.
"Can you help me please?" He asked me, almost in a whisper, as if he was anxious about asking me. I smiled and nodded.
"I will" I told him.

My brother came back downstairs with the original paper

and a note pad. William slipped back under the desk and handed them to me.

"Sorry Kaleb, I have to read this" I explained.

"It's okay. I'm looking forward to tonight" Kaleb admitted.

"Why, what's going on tonight?" William asked, looking at me.

"If school are okay with it, I'm going to Freddy's tonight. You know, to get to know him a bit more" Kaleb explained.

"Why would you want to do that?" William teased. I stuck my tongue out at him.

"I know you'll have a great time. I promise you, there's not one person in the world I trust more than Freddy" William admitted. I smiled and thanked him.

"This is where you say the same about me!" William told me. "You know I trust you".

"I still don't get why you're not stopping at mine tonight, we had it all planned out" William admitted. I looked at him and then at my watch.

"Right. Am I okay to look at everything in about half an hour please? I think William needs to talk" I asked Mrs Just politely. She smiled.

"Yeah sure, I'll just take Kaleb around the college, it has some photos he'll love" She replied. The two went off. I lead my brother out of the shop, locked the shop up and we went into the toilets. I checked it was empty. I sat on the edge of the sinks. He sat beside me.

"Okay, go ahead and ask whatever you want. I'll answer any questions the best I can" I told William.

"Why aren't you stopping with us tonight?" He asked.

"Because your Mum and Dad wanted to spend the night watching some things on T.V. or Netflix with you" I told him.

"We could do that with you there? Aren't you family?" He asked, his voice getting a bit high.
I smiled.

"Of course, but I understand why they want to do this. They've looked after you for the past ten years and want a night where it's just like old times. I think you'll have a great time by what I hear they have planned!" I reassured him.
"I want a night like old times too. Like when I would call Ben up every night to say good night, like when we would beg my Mum and Dad to let us go to town together on our own..." William cried. He wiped his eyes with the back of his hands.

I sighed and pulled my phone out of my pocket.
"I was going to save this...but I think this is the time to do it" I said quietly.
"What is it?" William sobbed. I set the phone up.
"Once I've left, press play. Just remember, we all love you and want to help you. Please don't hide it from us. I'll be back in once it has finished" I told him. I walked out.

William looked as the door closed. He stared at my phone. He pressed play. A familiar face popped up.
"Hi William, I saw Freddy's phone laying here. He's left it here whilst you both popped out and decided to do this" Ben Started. "I just wanted to say some things as I know I won't be able to say them when I...It happens" Ben said in the video.

William sniffled.
"You are my best friend in the world, and I will always be with you...Wait, that sounds a bit creepy?" He continued.
William laughed.
"Anyway, it might seem at times like your family are doing

things that don't seem right to you. Just trust them. Amy...Barry...Freddy... They will be trying to help you but are blind. They are trying to find a pea in a pitch-black warehouse" Ben said through the phone.

"Our...bond...was perfect and huge so it will devastate everyone seeing us torn apart. Although we weren't going out in the way most people thought, there was a bigger thing called brotherhood. It is your job to look after all of them for us. Do what they ask, chances are, it isn't just for your benefit. Just like you, they might not be able to admit if they need or are feeling something, especially since they'll know you are going through enough yourself" Ben explained.

"I can hear footsteps, likely yours, likely Freddy's or maybe a horse that's just walking by" Ben joked. It made William laugh quite hard. I smiled from outside the door. I stopped a fellow student from going in and explained that something was being dealt with.
"I guess all there is left to say is: Thanks for being my best friend, I have treasured every minute of it and if I had to choose between still being alive or meeting you, I wouldn't change a thing. Just remember, make me proud and laugh like you have done since we met. One last thing: Good night William!" Ben told him; Ben smiled before cutting the camcorder off.

William smiled, sobbed, laughed all at once. He leant against the mirror for a few minutes.
He took a deep breath before coming out, the phone still in his hand. I nearly fell into the room. I caught my balance. William wrapped his arms around me. I did the same.
"I'm going to do what my parents have planned" He told me. I let go of him and smiled understandingly.

"That's good. And I'll try and help your friend" I told William.
"If anyone can help him, you can" My brother told me, with
a smile.

"What do you wanna do now, it's up to you?" I asked him
patiently. He thought.
"Can we continue as normal?" He asked. I nodded and
motioned for him to follow me back to the repair shop.
Mrs Just and Kaleb were at a table close to the booth. Mrs
Just stood up when she saw us whilst Kaleb remained
seated. I quickly opened the shutter and followed William
inside.
"Everything okay guys?" She asked with concern.

We exchanged glances.
"It will be, in time" William said with a small smile.
Kaleb and William spoke whilst I looked at the pad William
had brought down with him. It had instructions, suggestions,
and other lists on it. I discussed these with the teaching
assistant before asking her to fill in one of the shop's forms.

"By the way, I've spoken through Kaleb's and your plan with
the school AND his Dad and they like the idea. His Dad
asked me to give you his number. He said to tell him what
time to drop him off and ring him when he wants picking
up as long it's before 8p.m." Mrs Just informed me. I smiled
and thanked her. Kaleb overheard and smiled himself. It was
great to see him smile; I knew it was rare he did nowadays.

"Does his Dad want to meet me first, just to make sure he
knows I'm a good person?" I asked. She shook her head.
"He knows about you. Kaleb told him you helped him and
William from a group of bullies the other week. We have
also of course verified you are a kind and compassionate
person. Plus...He's said that it's unusual Kaleb would ask to

go to someone else's house, so you must have a good aura!" Mrs Just explained. "Plus, he told me he's busy today until home time. He did say he wants to meet you though and will when he drops Kaleb off and picks him up". I nodded.

"Are you sure you wanna do this?" I asked Kaleb. He looked at me.
"I do. I'm nervous but yeah, I'm also kind of excited" Kaleb admitted.
"Have you been to my house before?" I asked him. He shook his head.
"Then of course you are going to be nervous about it. That's nothing to be ashamed of. I will make sure we have a good time which will help you to feel more comfortable around me" I told him. He smiled and stuck his hand out slowly. I saw looks of surprise on William's and Mrs Just's faces. I extended my hand and lightly shook his hand.

23

It was now 1:15p.m. and we were in the classroom with my fellow students.

"Good afternoon, we have a guest with us this week. This is Freddy's brother William. He's here to see how we work and how Freddy doesn't" Danny cracked. I rolled my eyes. Everyone laughed.

"Now, mainly for William's benefit but also to refresh our minds, I wanted to go back to the basics of computer repair for this lesson. William, as one of my students for this week, if you have any questions that you feel could be at your level, please do ask" Danny encouraged William and explained to the others. William nodded.

"Let's start off small. William, what's the difference between a netbook and a laptop?" Danny asked my brother. He thought for a moment.

"I think the main difference is the size. Netbooks tend to be smaller and less expensive. I'm guessing Netbooks have less storage space and features too but aren't sure about that?" William answered.

Danny smiled.

"Yep, you're right. Well done! A netbook is in fact a generic name given for a small, lightweight, and inexpensive laptop. They are quite often used by people who just need to complete small, light tasks like email, internet browsing and maybe light entertainment" Danny confirmed.

"What's the difference between a netbook and a notebook" Danny asked, mainly looking at William.

"Erm, I think netbooks and even laptops are often referred to as notebooks so there isn't much of a difference" William suggested. Danny nodded and smiled. William did too. I gave my brother a high five.

"Okay smarty pants, what's the difference between the writeable discs: DVD R and DVD RW?" Danny asked William with a smile on his face. I could tell he was surprised how smart William was.

"I'm gathering one you can rewrite as many times as you want whereas the other once you burn on to it, it's locked. This means if you mess up on the settings or anything on the latter, the disc is useless" William thought out loud. Danny came forward and gave William a high five himself. "Yep well done!" He congratulated William.

"But if that's the case, why don't people just use the one which you can rewrite as many times as they wanted?" William asked.

"Well, the price is a major factor. The DVD R, which you can only write on once is often fifty percent cheaper for twice the number of discs! So even if you messed up a couple of times, you'd still have lots of spare discs to use" Danny explained.

"Now this one is hard William so don't worry if you don't know it: What is the difference between a virus and malware?" Danny asked him. William thought for 20 seconds before shaking his head.

"Finally, I can catch him out!" Danny joked. We all laughed. "Malware is an umbrella term so actually a computer virus IS malware. Other forms of Malware include spyware, adware, worms, and trojans" Danny explained.

"Has a trojan got anything to do with the story of the trojan horse?" William asked. Danny smiled faintly.

"Yep, a trojan like many forms of malware takes advantage of your trust to cause more problems or even increase the amount of Malware on your computer. Like with the Trojan horse, it was seemingly a gift. They let it in and then they were all killed that night by soldiers hiding inside. A trojan is a file infested with lots of rubbish and damaging things to your computer system. Why do you think people are fooled to download these?" Danny explained and asked William.

"Because they put them inside files named after popular things like songs, videos and apps?" William asked.

"Yes!" Danny said. He gave William a piece of paper. It turned out to be a small voucher for a local sweet shop up the road.

The rest of the college day went well, and William shockingly kept up despite being six years younger than the youngest regular student on the course! Amy came and picked us up at around 3:15p.m.

"Are you sure you don't mind it being just William, Barry and me tonight?" Amy asked. I smiled and shook my head.

"I completely understand. Besides, I'm helping one of William's friends tonight at Uncle Andy's" I told Amy. She smiled and thanked me. Amy dropped me off at Uncle Andy's before they drove off towards their house. I could see them waving, I waved back.

I walked into the house. Uncle Andy was getting ready to go out. He was in his bedroom, straightening his suit out.

"Hi Uncle Andy!" I greeted him.

"Hey Freds, how are you?" Uncle Andy asked.

"I'm okay thanks. Would it be okay for a pupil from

William's school to come here tonight whilst you are out? I'm covering his TA after the Easter Holidays, but he's got some confidence issues and is very quiet so I'm going to try and help him as much as I can" I explained.

Uncle Andy nodded.
"Look at you, the mentor" He grinned. I laughed.
"He's a great kid, he just doesn't realise it. He's friends with William. I met him when I saved them both from a group of bullies in the school playground" I informed him.
"What's his name?".
"Kaleb" I replied.
"As long as he and his Dad does know that I will be out, so it'll just be you and him?" Uncle Andy said. I confirmed that we had told them.

I waved Uncle Andy off has he got into a taxi. Uncle Andy waved back and shouted that he hopes everything goes well. I thanked him before going in to sort a few things out before my guest arrived. I got paper and stationery ready as well as my laptop in case we needed it for anything. I still was not exactly sure on how to help Kaleb yet but was sure I would find a way quickly. There was a knock on the door about half an hour later.

24

I went downstairs and opened the door. In front of me was Kaleb and a man just younger than Barry. He must have been in his 30's.

"Freddy?" The guy asked. I smiled and nodded.

"Yeah, Freddy Lewis. I'm guessing your Kaleb's Dad"

"Yes! My name's Dillon. Kaleb's told me about you, so has the school" He told me.

"I dread to think" I joked. He laughed.

"No, it's been really good. I think I should just leave you both to it for now as I don't want to drag it out for Kaleb's sake! We will meet properly another time. That's if you are both happy with that" The Dad said. I nodded and looked at the boy beside him. I could see he was really nervous but excited. After all, for him, this was an epic adventure!

"I'll see you later Dad!" Kaleb told him, giving him a hug.

"See you later son and like I said to Mrs Just, just give me a ring when he wants to come home. Unless I hear before, I'll get here for about 8p.m. It's a half an hour's drive" Dillon told us. I nodded. We waved Dillon off from the door then we were on our own.

"Well done for coming. That was really brave of you" I told him. He smiled.

"Can I have some water please?" He asked. I could hear by his voice that his throat was dry. I smiled and asked him to follow me to the kitchen.

"Do you want anything else to drink: Juice, milk, pop?" I offered.

"What kind of milk?" He enquired.

"Green top, which is semi skimmed. It's all I can drink" I told him.

"Can I have some milk please?" He asked.
"Of course! I have to say, you are very polite!" I observed.
Kaleb just nodded. I poured him some milk. I then showed him where the toilets were, the escape routes and a room he could use as a quiet room if he needed a minute to himself.

We went up to my room. He sat on the floor in front of my bed. I came away from my desk where I had planned for us to sit. I brought everything to the floor and sat with him.
"What are your plans then?" He asked.
"I don't have any plans, apart from getting to know you some more and trying to help you to feel more comfortable. That way, I'll be able to support you better when I'm your temporary TA" I explained to him.
"Thanks for doing this" He told me. I smiled.
"My pleasure. So, what would you like to do?" I asked.

We spent half an hour revising on his favourite subject: Maths! He was happy when I admitted it had always been my favourite too, as well as I.C.T.
"Kaleb. I just remembered what you were saying at the college earlier?" I started.
He looked up at me.
"You said that your quirks are crazy?" I recalled. He looked down.
"Well, some of them are weird" He admitted.
"Well, try telling me one of them?" I suggested, with a kind smile on my face. He looked at me for a moment.
"I'm really fussy about food for one. My ham as to come from ASDA and my cheese has to come from Iceland" Kaleb told me.

I put a hand lightly on his thin shoulders to calm him.
"So, they taste different to you so of course you would

prefer the ones you liked better" I reasoned. After all, who hasn't got a tale on food. Like I hate apples but love apple juice!

"I tell you what, can you tell me the 'quirk' which you think is the worst or most embarrassing?" I asked him. He hesitated as he thought about it.

We spent about 15 minutes talking about what makes us unique.

"Look, we all have things that make us different, even if we don't admit it. It would be so dull if everyone were the same and liked the same things! Like people look at me funnily when I say I don't like Apples but like Apple juice" I told Kaleb.

We talked about the quirk he felt was the weirdest. It was not anything dangerous so told him that it was nothing to feel bad about.

"Sometimes, it makes things clearer when we remind ourselves why we like or don't like these specific things" I said.

"I guess I like to laugh and to make others laugh too" Kaleb told me.

"That's really good. I bet you can do that in other ways too just by being yourself. Although that ways okay too as long as the other person is happy with it too" I assured him.

"I think it's the texture of an apple I hate and of course, that texture isn't in the juice" I explained.

"I tell you what: Let's do some more revision-But want to make it a challenge?" I asked him with a smile on my face. He nodded with anticipation. We spent another half an hour revising different subjects our way. I think Kaleb did really well, with the revision, concentration, and his confidence.

We then played some games on my tablet. Another of Kaleb's hidden talents is Angry Birds! In one minute, he was beating high scores that had taken me days to get! He stuck his tongue out at me. I smiled at him.

"Well done. Look how much more confident you've become in one night!" I praised him.

"I couldn't have done it without you" Kaleb said.

"We all need help with something. With me, it's knowing or being encouraged to have some fun. Sometimes, I think life is all about learning" I admitted to him.

"That doesn't sound so bad. Look what you've become" Kaleb said. I laughed.

"Yeah but it does affect friendships and does make you more of a target for nasty people" I admitted.

"So, what are you saying, to change who we are to suit others?"

I looked up at him.

"You're right" I admitted. "We shouldn't ever do that".

"You were bullied?" Kaleb asked curiously. I nodded.

"How did you deal with it?" He asked.

"Well for a start, not everything will work in all cases of course. I dealt with it by mostly trying to ignore them, of course, sometimes...or often...it really hurt me inside. Not once did I hit them or lower myself down to their level. That is what bullies want...That's how we win. You'll see" I told him. He smiled.

It was now just after 7p.m. and I could see that Kaleb was getting tired.

"Do you want to continue this another day. I think you're getting tired" I offered.

"No, I'm not!" He protested. I then went on my laptop and played a video.

Kaleb stared at me with evil eyes, I laughed.
The video was entitled: 'Yawning!'
About halfway through the video, he gave up and let the yawn out. But then I yawned too. We both laughed. I had done the same thing on a cousin during a sleepover, so I knew what the result would be!

It also proved I was covering up how tired I was too! I gave his Dad and ring and explained that Kaleb was getting tired and if we could pick this up another time. Dillon picked his son up about 40 minutes later, where they both thanked me for agreeing to support Kaleb. I smiled.
"It's my pleasure, he's so polite and kind" I told his Dad.
"I'm glad to hear it, it's how he's been brought up. Even though he's got special needs, he knows he still needs to watch his behaviour when possible and be kind" Dillon explained with a smile. I nodded. They were gone by 7:50p.m.

25

It was now the following day. I met William outside of the college. He smiled when he saw me.

"Hey, how did it go last night?" He asked me.

"Really well. I think Kaleb is becoming even more comfortable around me. I know that this will help when I'm assisting him after the Easter Holidays", I told my brother, "How did it go with you guys last night?".

"We had a great time. We watched a couple of films on Netflix then Mum tucked me in to bed. To be honest, I think she's finding it hard too. She hasn't tucked me in like that for around two years, unless I have had a nightmare, of course" William explained. "But to be honest, I liked how she did so last night".

"Sounds like we all had fun. Are you ready to have me back?" I joked. He laughed.

"Are you?" He teased.

We walked to the college room.

"Hi guys. Now, after yesterday, I wanted the class to fill in some refresher worksheets and I want William to do so too. Your knowledge and performance yesterday were remarkable!" Danny told us and praised William. William smiled; I think he loves it when people admit how smart he is! We spent the morning filling in the worksheets and taking a couple of tiny breaks.

It was now Lunchtime. William and I, of course, sat together to eat. I got a plain cheeseburger whilst my brother got a hot dog and blathered it in ketchup!

"People are going to think it's someone's arm you've cut off!" I warned.

"Don't give me any ideas" William replied. I laughed.

"Well, isn't it the most hated duo?" A voice said behind us. Even I recognised the voice. William's eyes shot wide open. "When they said you needed to move classes, they meant a nursery" Annabel scoffed cruelly at William.
"Leave William alone!" I demanded.
"Why, what are you going to do?"
"You actually expect me to lower myself down to your level. That's not going to happen as William, and I have more dignity in our little fingers than you do in your entire body!" I declared to her. She laughed.
"Where's your friend William?" Annabel asked, with a crooked grin.

My eyes shot open now. I knew who she was talking about by the tone of her voice and knew immediately that she was just evil!
"Kaleb is at School" William said. He had not caught on. Part of me was glad, and that part of me was my heart.
I stood up.
"Look, leave us alone, okay. This is getting more serious than bullying now and if you want me to take it further..." I shot back at her.

"You're a wimp" She said to me.
"Takes one to know one. Having to pick fights with people who you think are wimps" I said back at her.
"I also know who your Dad is so unless he would like everyone to read what his daughter is like all over the papers, I suggest you back off!" I challenged.

I had heard that her Dad was a politician-Whose main campaign was about anti-bullying!
Annabel now cowered back a bit.

"This includes staying away from Me, William and Kaleb" I made myself clear. She ran off.

William stared back at me.
"That felt so good!" I declared, taking a seat again.
"Are you sure that was such a good idea. What about if she reports you and twists your words?" William asked.
"Don't worry, this café is swamped with cameras...Plus Danny is under the computer repair shop counter...trying to hide from us" I said, shouting the last bit. Danny popped up.

"Oh, hi guys, how are you doing?" He said.
"knock it off, I know you was listening to every word" I declared.
"Don't worry about it, I saw and heard everything. You were using appropriate defence methods to protect you and your brother, who you are kind of responsible for whilst in College. I will put a note on your records to say what went on and why" Danny explained.
William and I exchanged glances and thanked him.
"One thing, next time she decides to pick on either of you, you need to tell me immediately, and I will take appropriate action alongside her school. Try not to threaten people if you can get away from the situation" Danny told us. I nodded in agreement. Danny walked away.

"She didn't mean Kaleb...Did she?" William asked. I shook my head.
"I'm sorry but Ben will be really proud of how you handled it" I reassured my brother.
"That's only because I didn't know who she meant"
"Deep down, I know you did. Your mind and heart just refused to believe someone could be that evil!" I told him. He nodded.
"Thanks for sticking up for me" William said gratefully. "Also,

for Kaleb". I smiled.

"You're both great boys with good hearts. Besides...I know..." I started.

William looked at me.

"Were you Bullied?" He asked.

"Yes" I admitted.

"So that's what you meant by 'that felt so good' after you had stood up to her!" William recalled. I nodded.

"To be honest, I only stood up to her as she was picking on you too. That's what I've always seemed to do, stand up for others but not myself. Still feels good when I do though!" I told him.

"Thanks again and I'll be there to stand up for you too. That's what brothers are for" William said.

"As well as annoy each other?" I joked.

"If you like?" He teased. We both laughed.

Miss Rodgers came into the café and asked to speak with me. I saw Peter coming up. Peter talked to William while I spoke to the teacher.

"Hi Freddy, what happened with Annabel? She's just reported you for bullying her, I'm almost certain this isn't true, but I have to check" Miss Rodgers informed me.

"What! She was picking on William and me, she even asked him where Ben was", I told the teacher. Her eyes burst open.

"Oh god. The whole class knows about what happened to Ben as I paid tribute to him in class the other day! Can I ask you to tell me as closely as you can what you said to her?" Miss Rodgers remarked.

"I just asked...or told her to stay away from me, William and Kaleb, as I was informed last night that she has been picking on Kaleb more than everyone thinks" I explained.

She nodded.

"She mentioned something about you threatening her Dad?" She asked. I put my face in my hands.

"What she was referring to is after she had asked where Ben was, I had to resort to threatening to go to the papers about her behaviour. I tried everything else and I could tell she was really hurting William" I admitted.

"Right. Would you say there were any trustworthy witnesses who heard and saw everything, who would tell me everything including what you and William did and said?" Miss Rodgers asked.

"Danny heard everything whilst sorting the repair shop out. He had tried to hide from William and me, but I had already seen him" I explained.

"Your tutor, Danny?" She clarified. I nodded.

"Is he in his office?".

"I think so, he went in that direction. If not, he could be in the classroom just further along preparing for the next lesson" I told the teacher. She thanked me.

"Now, if she bothers you or anyone you are responsible for again, I am giving you permission to record it for evidence, so we may take it further. You must surrender this immediately and not show it to anyone else but the School, the Police, and the college. Then you MUST report it to either me or Danny as soon as you can. You must not take matters in your own hands, as if you did, it could be classed as slander!" Miss Rodgers warned me. I explained that we had already promised Danny we would tell him next time. She nodded before walking off to find Danny.

After we got in from college, Barry and Amy went for a night out together, so it was just me and William. We were, of course, at their house. We messed about and listened to music. I also found out that he was nearly as strong as me. To be honest, that is not such a big achievement! William spent a bit of the evening looking up more about computers.

The whole week went well, and William continued to learn more about a subject that was well beyond his years! Danny was very shocked, as was the class including me! Danny ended up giving us a document offering William a place on his new Youth Computing Programme once he becomes 13. Now it was the Tuesday of the following week. It was of course the Easter holidays. Uncle Andy and I were in London to attend my passport interview. There is a HM Passport Centre in Portsmouth, but they did not have any appointments due to shorter opening hours.

We were walking to the centre after a bite to eat at a local café.
"You feeling okay about this interview?" Uncle Andy asked me.
"Yeah I think so" I replied.
"They will just ask you questions like where you've lived, who you live with, what you do and stuff like that" Uncle Andy explained.
"But I'm adopted?".
"That's why we've had to bring extra paperwork for you. We explained that in your application too. All this should help speed things up" Uncle Andy told me.

We arrived at the centre, checked in at the reception and took a seat in the waiting area. We waited for about 15 minutes before someone came over.
"Hello, are you 'Freddy Lewis'?" She asked. I nodded. She smiled and shook my hand.
"Would you mind coming to the desk on your own?" She

asked. I shook my head.

"Just to let you know that I am adopted so Uncle Andy will know more about some aspects of that than I will" I explained.
"That is not a problem. Is this your Uncle?".
"Yeah. I am Andy Lewis. I have also gathered some extra paperwork for you guys" Uncle Andy introduced himself, giving the interviewer the documents.
"That is good thank you. So, would you like to come over Freddy" She asked. I nodded.

The interview lasted around half an hour and most of the questions were easy and straight forward. If I did not know the answer, we just moved on to the next one. I stood up, shook her hand again and joined Uncle Andy. We then caught the train back to Portsmouth from London Waterloo Station. We were home for 4p.m. I was stopping at Uncle Andy's tonight and we had cut it down to twice a week. From next week, I would not sleep here, but would see him once a week, Other times I would video call with him.

Uncle Andy and I watched some films including E.T and Total Recall whilst eating Dominoes Pizzas and eating the last buns we had in. We went to our rooms around 11p.m., as we were tired by this time.

26

I woke up. I felt refreshed and ready for the day. I went and had some cereal with Uncle Andy.

"Hey Freds" He said, turning to see me enter the kitchen.

"Hey! How long have you been up?" I asked. He laughed.

"Well, I wanted to finish one last thing I had to do for work now so that I could relax before I go to the Czech Republic" He explained. I nodded.

"Are you sure you're okay about me going?" Uncle Andy asked.

"I know it's going to be so tough and weird you not being here but, in time..." I told my Uncle. "Besides, you've got your other kids in Czech Republic. I've got William to annoy me".

Uncle Andy laughed.

I caught the bus to nearby William's street and walked the rest of the way. The sun and wind were just the right ratio for me. I knocked on the door. Amy answered it.

"I've told you, just come in. You're family!" She said, closing the door behind me.

"I will do, it's just going to take some time getting used to doing it" I promised. She smiled understandingly.

"How was Uncle Andy?" Amy asked.

"He was great thanks. He's getting ready to go".

"And how are you holding up with that?" She asked.

"Surprisingly, I feel okay, obviously I'm sad he's going but those kids need him in the same way I needed him" I replied.

I went upstairs and put my bags near my bed. I checked my phone; William was still asleep at 10a.m.! I then noticed something suspicious. I sat at the foot of his bed. I took my pinkie finger and traced it around his foot. William immediately started giggling and pulled his foot away.

"Damn, how did you know?" He asked.

"You are as good at keeping a straight face as I am, you were grinning your head off!" I revealed. He shook his head. He rubbed his foot.

"Are you okay, did I scratch you?" I checked my nails. He shook his head and laughed.

"It's an itch" He explained. I laughed too.

"You know what they say though, so you'd better watch yourself" William remarked.

"And what's that then?" I asked.

"Only give what you can take!" William teased. I stuck my tongue out at him. I knew I would be looking over my shoulder and sleeping with one eye open for the next week!

Turns out William had been awake for around three hours, so he had had his breakfast, gotten his wash, and done some of his chores. He had then gotten back into some clean pyjamas and back into bed just to prank me. I was happy that I had caught on very quick! We both went downstairs.

"Ah, so did you catch Freddy out then?" Amy asked William. He shook his head, I laughed.

"No, I noticed him grinning" I told her. She laughed.

"What do you say about me and you two going to a shopping centre and just having a look around?" She asked.

"Please can it be the city centre; I love the Cascades Shopping Centre!" William said.

"That one's my favourite!" I admitted.

"I guess that's two to one" Amy conceded defeat.

"Wait, where did you want to go?" I asked her.

"The one near the Spinnaker Tower, I thought we could go

in and maybe have a meal too" Amy explained. I thought for a moment.

"Why don't we do both. Spend some time at Cascades then go on to Gunwharf and the Spinnaker Tower?" William reasoned. I nodded. Amy smiled.

"That's a great idea!" Amy exclaimed. William gave me a high five.

The three of us got into the car.

"Where's Barry?" I asked.

"He's gone to work; this is my day off" Amy explained.

We spent around an hour in Cascade Shopping Centre and the adjoining shopping street, Commercial Road. I got some rum balls from Hilbornes sweet shop inside Cascades.

"Hey William, try one of these!" I suggested. He did so. He pulled a face but then relaxed and chewed some more.

"It's actually very good, once you get by the taste explosion that first hits you" He observed. I laughed.

"I've gotten used to it and barely notice anymore!" I explained. We went back and got him some as well.

As agreed, we then got back into the car and drove to the Gunwharf Quays Shopping Centre. It was about 1p.m.

"As you might have guessed, it's mostly clothes shops here so if you two want to go to the waterside for a while, that's fine with me. Just keep your phones on you and don't go too far" Amy said. We nodded.

Whilst she went looking in all the clothes shops, my brother and I went straight down to the waterfront. There were barriers all around to stop people falling in. We looked out. The weather was still fantastic. It was quite busy since it was the school holidays for just under two more weeks.

"Hey, what are you guys doing here?" A woman asked. Miss Rodgers.

"Hi Miss Rodgers! Mum's just looking in the clothes shops" William told his teacher. She smiled.

"Good to see you both getting fresh air. It is often really nice weather in Portsmouth but some people, young and old, stay inside" Miss Rodgers commented.

"I know, I always like to go on my laptop, but I also make sure I get regular fresh air. Even if it's just a half hour of walking" I explained. She nodded.

"So how are you both doing, with the new arrangements and living together?" Miss Rodgers asked.

"I have really enjoyed living with them and William is annoying but cool" I joked.

"I've really liked having my brother here and larking about with him" William told her. Me and him exchanged glances.

"I am so glad it is working out!" The teacher told us with a big smile.

"There is another thing...I spoke to Danny as well as some other people who were in the canteen" Miss Rodgers informed us.

"They confirmed that you stood up for William. Whilst this was very loyal and kind of brave, I must warn you to be careful. This is what she could want, for you to snap and since you are an adult, it would be seen as worse, even though she is obviously provoking the matter. Annabel is known all around the city for being very difficult and she doesn't seem to discriminate who she's difficult for" Miss Rodgers explained.

"I'm sorry" I said.

"It's okay, the school understand, trust me, they do! BUT next time, take a deep breath and lead William away and go

straight to a member of staff" The teacher urged, "Besides, she won't be bullying you at school".
"What do you mean?" I asked.
"It might pee her Dad and some big people off, but we've expelled her for bullying and threatening behaviour. She isn't allowed in the school grounds" Miss Rodgers told us with a smile. We both thanked her for doing all this. She nodded and smiled.

Amy came across the path to us.
"Hi Miss Rodgers, is everything okay?" Amy asked. She nodded.
"As I was explaining to William and Freddy, we have taken further action about that girl bullying and harassing William" Miss Rodgers told Amy. William put his hands up to his face.
"What girl?" Amy demanded.
"William or Freddy didn't tell you...Did they?" The teacher asked, just realising.
Amy shook her head.
"I told Barry, I just didn't want to worry you needlessly as the school and me were dealing with it" I explained.
"But it didn't work?" She asked.
"No, she's started harassing and being mean to me too. It is being sorted though! Miss Rodgers has just said the girl has been expelled" I reassured Amy. She nodded.

"I'm not happy about not being told about this but I don't blame you. I can be overprotective sometimes" Amy admitted. "I will try and tone down and try to relax with you more. I don't want to be that kind of Mum where her son can't talk to his Mum about these things", she told William. William smiled and gave her a hug.

Miss Rodgers rushed off to get a new dress. Amy, William,

and I went across the way to the Spinnaker Tower, a famous landmark of Portsmouth.

"I haven't actually been in here" I admitted.

"Neither have I, I'm scared of heights!" William admitted.

Amy smiled and led us both in. We just explained that we just wanted to get something to eat from the café first and they showed us through.

We all had a great time. Me and William got a breakfast while Amy got some pasta. I received a text.

'Can you come as soon as possible please?' Uncle Andy had sent.

27

I showed Amy the message and we rushed out. Amy ran back and paid the bill. We pulled outside Uncle Andy's home 15 minutes later.

I went inside to the living room whilst Amy and William waited in the kitchen.
"Hi Freds" Uncle Andy said.
"What's going on?" I asked. Uncle Andy shook his head sadly.
"I'm leaving for the Czech Republic on Friday" He told me. I sighed.

"The kids' Mum has deteriorated and if there isn't someone there to take the kids when she passes, they'll be immediately put into the care system. If this happened, I might not get them back" Uncle Andy explained. I nodded.
"You need to do what you need to do" I remarked, "I'll be okay, everyone will make sure of that I'm sure".
Uncle Andy smiled slightly and gave me a long hug.

Uncle Andy then spoke to Amy in private whilst William and I sorted things to take back home with us. Uncle Andy had put some more boxes in my room. A removal van would bring the remaining bigger items the next day. The room looked lonely and sad. I sighed; William put a hand on my shoulder.

It was now the next day. I heard a honk. I went downstairs, William on my heels. Barry was waiting outside. Also, outside were two big guys unloading furniture out of a van. Barry came back in.
"Oh hi, do you want us to store this in the basement until

we're ready to sort them into their rooms?" He asked me. I nodded. I remained in the kitchen with William and Peter, who had just come by. I had spoken to Kaleb via video call earlier and he seemed to be looking forward to school the week after next and having me as his assistant. I was looking forward to helping someone and doing something different.

"I want to watch Despicable Me!" William said. I rolled my eyes. It was now that evening.
"We have watched that for the past few nights I've stopped here!" I complained.
"Got any better suggestions?" He challenged. I thought hard. After a minute, I clicked my fingers and rushed over to the bags I had brought back yesterday. I dug through them.
"William, you like Goosebumps, right?" I asked. He nodded.
"Yeah" He said.
"Have you ever seen the T.V. Series?" I asked. He thought and shook his head.
"Do you want to give it a go, I've got the complete set right here!" I suggested. He nodded enthusiastic.
"Great, it was made in the 1990's, so the effects might not be up to date and some sections might be a bit jumpy" I warned him. He nodded and smiled.
We spent that night watching the Goosebumps T.V. Series. We fell asleep sometime during the second episode of the second season.

28

I was sat in the car with Barry, Amy, William, and Peter. Now, the moment was upon us-The day Uncle Andy was leaving! We were heading to Stansted Airport. Peter wanted to come along and see if he could provide me further support. He also wanted to meet Uncle Andy before he went. I was terribly upset but felt incredibly supported and knew everything was going to be fantastic.

I got out of the car. Danny was also there waiting to see him off. Sure enough, ten minutes later, a car came around the corner and into the car park. One of the neighbours had given him a lift. They said farewell before the car drove off.

Uncle Andy stood staring at us for a few minutes, we were all lined up. He came towards us.
"I'm going to another country, not another planet" He joked. We all laughed.
"Thanks for coming to see me off" He said, returning to being serious.
"Where else would we be?" I asked. He smiled.
He said goodbye to everyone one by one, then met Peter.

Finally, He stepped up to me.
"It's been an honour watching you grow both by size and as a person. Well done for handling this so well and we will still speak lots" He said, getting a bit tearful.
"I know" I said. I was trying to hold it together. He stared at me. I just could not.

Uncle Andy put his arms around me and squeezed me. He always used to do that a lot when I was younger. I laughed.
"Goodbye Freds" Uncle Andy said. I nodded and gave him

one last hug.

"I...will...be...right...here..." He said, pointing to my head. I burst out laughing. He was obviously referring to E.T, one of our favourite films we always watched together.

"Goodbye" I said, gathering myself together and referencing Elliot's reply.

He stepped back and walked towards the airport entrance, with William and I following. We stopped at the doors. Uncle Andy flashed us one last wave before he was gone. The doors closed slowly. My shoulders sagged. William wrapped his arms around me. It made me feel stronger straight away. I put my arm around his shoulders. I led him away from the doors and back to the adults.

We neared everyone else.

"Everything is going to be just fine" Barry said.

"It won't be, but it will be soon" I corrected him with a small smile.

Danny smiled.

"You really have grown" He told me. I laughed.

"It's because of you, all of you. Being there and supporting me when my uncle couldn't" I admitted.

"Where else would we be" Peter repeated. I nodded.

"It's mostly down to you though" I said, looking at William. He looked back at me.

"How?".

"When I met you, I learnt new ways of handling things and coping with changes, you too" I explained. He let out a few tears. I and everyone else laughed.

"Git" William said, trying to wipe the tears away.

"That's not nice!" I teased. He stuck his tongue out.

We all walked back to our cars and left the airport in a line.

It was now the following Monday. Amy drove me and William to Milton Park Primary School. She pulled the car up to the side of the road.

"Ready?" William turned to ask me.

"Yep, let's start this" I replied. We both got out and Amy drove off towards work.

William led me towards the visitor's entrance. Miss Rodgers had given William permission to come in with me, so he could show me to where I needed to be.

"Hi Freddy!" Miss Rodgers said, coming out of a storeroom.

"Hi" I returned the greeting.

"You still don't mind doing this? It is a huge help" Miss Rodgers admitted. I nodded.

"I'm looking forward to learning new things and helping Kaleb".

"You have already been doing both from what I've heard" Miss Rodgers told me. I laughed.

"There is always something new to learn, no matter how smart you are" I replied, referencing what Ben had told me. Miss Rodgers smiled.

William went to the breakfast club whilst Miss Rodgers, the headmistress and the SENCO had a meeting with me to discuss exactly what they wanted me to do with Kaleb and how. I explained the meeting between me and him at my house had helped me to understand him and his needs a bit more. They also confirmed fully on what I should do if we happened to see Annabel again. They seemed very happy with me. Miss Rodgers gave me what I would need to assist Kaleb in the first lesson. Mostly paperwork, worksheets, and booklets. Miss Rodgers went straight to her classroom whilst I joined William in the hall. I had some toast and jam.

At around 8:45a.m., we made our way to the classroom

where we met Kaleb. I gave Kaleb a high five.
"Come on in" Miss Rodgers called from inside. William, Kaleb, and I exchanged glances. I motioned with my hand for them to lead the way. As we walked into the classroom, I could not help but wonder where this week...This month...This new chapter would lead.

The End

About Me

Hi, my name is Shane and I live in Hull, U.K. I have been trying to write stories since I was 10. I have got development problems which is why it has taken me so long to write a story good enough to be published. I was later diagnosed with Autism, ADHD and learning difficulties. I'm also an disability advocate and volunteer with numerous disability groups and settings including Castaway and Kingsmill.

I wrote Freddy, as if I would cast myself as him. Although I love being different, I just wanted to be someone else for once, if that makes sense?
The autistic side of me has been put into Kaleb and I do share a lot of his quirks. I also loved Maths and I.C.T.! The tutu picture was not entirely made up either...

I am a big Goosebumps and Shivers fan! :D My main non-quirky fascination is bus information. I know lots about the bus services of Hull!

I have two brothers called Harry and Billy. Harry is the most annoying, but Billy is catching up! XD
I love them both to pieces and they make me a better person, as do all my family and friends.

The sentence near the start, where I use the music artist 'Hardwell' to describe how my voice dropped, is not a dig at him. He is, in fact, one of my favourite DJ's and producers! I love a wide range of music. This includes: Queen, ABBA, Hardwell, Scooter, Mike Williams, Steve Aoki, Avicii and many more. I used to be in the choir at Primary School, but my vocal cords dropped and did not have the courage to pick them back up.

Special thanks to:
- Frankeet11 (YouTube) and your Mum: For being the first person to proof-read the original story. Thanks Buddy!
- The Wallet Kids: For making my new book cover. I love it! Thanks guys! Find them on Instagram and Facebook: @thewalletkids. Thanks to Edith for also checking my book and notifying me about the corrections needed.
- My Family, Friends, CatZero, Hull FC, Kingsmill School and Manor Farm: For your encouragement & support!
- All who read this story: For giving my story a try and I really hope you enjoyed reading!

Connect with me:
- Email: relate.shanestoneley@gmail.com.
- Instagram, Facebook and YouTube: Shane's Autism & ADHD Journey.
- Amazon: www.amazon.co.U.K./shane-stoneley/e/B07HH8GZY5

Printed in Great Britain
by Amazon